THE SECRET 6:
HOUSE OF WALKING CORPSES

THE SECRET 6

HOUSE OF
WALKING CORPSES

By Robert J. Hogan

STEEGER BOOKS • 2020

CHAPTER 1
THE DEATH SHIP

THE FACE of the young man at the controls of the low-winged cabin plane was wrinkled in smiles until he sighted the strange picture of a small but palatial yacht drifting aimlessly in the middle of Long Island Sound.

His cold blue eyes hardened. The smile left his face to be replaced by a troubled frown.

He was flying the plane for the first time from a port near College Point. His whole body had thrilled with the flight, because it had been his first since he had been snatched from the electric chair on a framed charge of murder.

Doing nearly two hundred miles an hour, he had paid little attention to the drifting yacht when he first sighted it. At his speed it had seemed as though the craft were moving slowly.

But as he neared it, his trained eyes had failed to see the parting of waves before the bow. The yacht wasn't moving. Perhaps it was anchored while the occupants did some fishing.

The silent exhausts on his plane cut the noise of the giant motor down to a gentle hum as he neared the boat. Curiosity drove him on. There was something strange about the yacht which he couldn't quite figure out.

He lifted a pair of powerful binoculars and adjusted them to his eyes. Now he knew what it was. His mind's eye had seen it and registered it rather than his visible eye. And that something that he hadn't been able to explain before now gave the yacht an eerie look.

The flag was at half-mast.

"Queer," he said. "There's no one on deck. The boat looks deserted."

He swung the glasses and took a good look at the bow of the craft. An exclamation escaped his thin lips.

"It's drifting, too. They haven't even bothered to drop anchor."

He was much nearer now. He straightened a little as everything came into clearer view. Then his hand touched the throttle before him and the engine picked up more speed.

He cut the motor back and circled low about the drifting craft.

"The whole thing looks queer," he decided. "A yacht drifting. No one on board except a dead man—if I can believe the meaning of that flag at half-mast."

He frowned as he continued to study the yacht.

"Maybe it broke loose from the moorings somewhere."

Another good look at the bow.

"No, there's the anchor up on the forward deck. Someone would have seen it leaving a pier or dock. There ought to be ropes dragging."

Then his keen eyes took in something else. There should have been two boats, one on either side of the craft. The curved arms to hold them were visible, but one boat was gone. The ropes and tackles that had held it were swinging with the slight movement of the craft in the gentle ground swell.

Someone had left the yacht to drift, had taken off in one of those small life boats.

The young man swung about the yacht once more.

"That," he said, "is one of the queerest things he ever seen. Wonder what the rest of the band can figure out of it."

He turned his plane southward, gave her the gun for more speed. His eyes roved the shore line for the small field he intended to use as a tarmac.

The young man was known to his five associates as "King"— just King. They had chosen him as their leader. The leader of a little vagabond band of men from various walks of life. Men who had outlawed themselves to fight crime under the fitting title of "The Secret 6."

Criminals knew them only by that name. Six just men who were banded together against them. And criminals feared them far more than the strong arm of the law.

The police believed The Secret 6 band to be composed of

arch-criminals, not knowing that King himself was the son of one of the greatest detectives who ever lived and the nephew of a former police chief, both killed by crime guns.

King sighted the jungle, or hideout, of his little band. He sighted the location of it, rather, for the cabin, which was situated in the thick woods of northeastern Long Island, was beyond sight from either land or sea or air.

The narrow field on which he planned to land was nearby, hidden from the main highway by a thick wood.

He circled over the cabin to let the other five know that he was back. They would hear the soft sound of his exhausts and be on their way to the flying field to meet him.

But the thrill of returning with that new ship was already partly gone.

HE FLEW above the field in a wide circle. Two cars were running at high speed along the highway a half mile or more distant. It wouldn't do to let anyone see him landing.

So he circled again until those cars had passed from view.

Then he shut off the motor and drifted down to a smooth landing.

As he climbed from the cabin, a gigantic figure ran toward him from the wood.

He was well over six feet in height. His skin was jet black. His wild, bushy hair bobbed like tiny wire springs from every side of his head as he ran.

He was Luga, the giant black Zulu chieftain who had left a great circus to become the self-appointed slave and aide of King, who had once saved his life.

"Master," he called, "you all right?"

King smiled.

"Sure, I'm all right, Luga," he said. "You talk as if you didn't expect me to be. Anything wrong?"

"Everything all right if you are, Master," said the faithful black.

King frowned. "What's behind all this, Luga?" he demanded.

"You late, Master," said Luga. "Then we get word over short-wave radio from 'Flo the Fleecer.' She say she overhear men plan to kill you."

King's eyes widened.

"You don't tell me," he said. "You mean the police?"

"Luga not know. You come quick to cabin. Maybe she talk again."

King nodded. He made a final inspection of the plane to make sure that everything had been left as it should be, then turned to Luga.

"Give me a hand, Luga," he said. "We'll roll the ship under those trees so no one can spot it from the air."

Together they pushed the plane until the overhanging branches hid it from view. Then King stood off and smiled as he studied the ship with a last inspection.

"How's she look, Luga?" he asked.

"Luga think she like big shiny bird. Very nice, Master. But you hurry. They want to kill you. You hear, maybe."

King nodded and smiled tolerantly. He followed Luga through the woods.

"She'll travel like a scared hawk, too, big boy," he said. "I doubt if there are many planes that can trim her for speed."

Luga shot a glance at King as he moved ahead, down the trail that led from large tree to large tree.

"You brave, Master," the big black said. "You not afraid to die?"

King laughed.

"You know, big boy," he said, "when you've put in as many hours flying as I have, you get sort of hardened to death. You get to be a fatalist. That's a bird who believes that he won't be killed until his time comes. A buddy of mine used to put it pretty well. He said the boss of the universe turns over a new page in the book every day. And when your time comes, your name is on the right side of the new sheet. So on that day he just draws a line through your name on that page and writes it on the opposite page. And that's all there is to it."

Luga shook his head. King's grin broadened.

"Anything else happen at the cabin since I left?"

"No, Master. Luga think that enough."

They came upon the cabin suddenly. King pushed open the door and smiled at the four faces looking at him.

There was "the Doctor," a man of science and chemistry and medicine. A big, heavy-set fellow with hands like hams and shoulders like those of an ox.

There was "Shakespeare," a gray-haired actor who was a master of mimic and make-up.

"The Bishop," a merry, stout little man with more strength than fat and a twinkle in his eye.

And "the Key," a dapper young man of slight build with a

shady past and an ability to open any lock or safe that was ever made. The Key had valuable contacts with the beggars of the metropolitan area. It was through his distribution to friends of five short wave radio sets that the Doctor had invented and built that The Secret 6 received valuable information of the underworld. The Bishop had been instrumental in reforming the Key.

"Listen, kid," the Key piped as King entered, "did you know that the thugs got the finger on you?"

King nodded. "So Luga tells me," he answered.

"You returned safely with the plane," the Bishop said. "We heard you go over."

"Those exhausts are very quiet," said the Doctor. "I didn't figure it would be you because the plane didn't make enough noise. Sounded more like a truck on a main highway somewhere."

"I think she'll do the trick," King smiled. "But I had to pay out about all we got out of that last job. It leaves us pretty well broke except for a little gasoline money."

"I would rather hear you say," said the Bishop with a twinkle in his merry eyes, "that we received the money in payment for services, rather than say we got it from a job."

"Hell—I mean, goodness, Bishop," the Key cut in. "It don't make any difference whether you call it a "job" or a "service," just so we get the dough."

The Doctor advanced and took King's right hand in his own huge ones, turned it palm up.

"I've given the Bishop and the Key their last treatments for changing fingertips," he said. "Let's take a look at yours."

8

King held still. The Doctor nodded. "Another treatment with the electric needle ought to finish you up, too," he said.

He took an electric needle attached to a storage battery of his own making and began working over the lines of King's fingers at the edges of the tips.

While he worked, King talked.

"I saw something that's got me guessing," he said.

"And we heard something that has us wondering also," answered Shakespeare. "No harm has come to you, King, I trust?"

"No," said King, "but there's a yacht floating in the Sound."

"A yacht floating?" exclaimed the Key. "You mean we can have it if we pick it up?"

King laughed. "Not that easy," he told him. "It won't do us any good, Key, except that there may be something aboard that needs investigating. I don't think the yacht broke loose from a dock because there aren't any lines dragging."

"And you mean," demanded the Bishop, "there is no one on board?"

"Right," nodded King. "At least I couldn't see anyone. I circled around it twice. It's almost out of sight of land so that it would be seen only from passing ships. And there weren't any at the moment. Saw a couple of sails, miles off, but that was all. I've been trying to figure—"

He stopped short. For a voice, a rather husky and at the same time, sweet feminine voice, was coming over the short wave receiver that the Doctor had built to receive the calls from the short waved senders the Key had put out.

"Hello, everybody. Hello, King and your Secret 6. This is Flo the Fleecer. I'm calling to make sure that you understood me the first time. It's important. They're trying to get you, King."

"There she is again," whispered Shakespeare hoarsely.

"I overheard a couple of men in the Brown Shoe last night," Flo the Fleecer went on. "They were talking about getting you, King. They think you're somewhere on Long Island. They're planning to lay a trap for you. Be careful. They think they'll break up The Secret 6 if they get you."

CHAPTER 2
THE BLACK THROAT

THE DOCTOR finished his work and inspected King's fingertips.

"There," he said, "if they do get you, they can't be sure of it when they check with the police fingerprints."

King looked at his fingertips, rubbed them together, looked at them again. He had the fingertip lines now of another man. Lines that the Doctor had designed. He nodded and smiled.

"Nice work, Doctor," he said.

Flo the Fleecer was repeating her warning. Every man in the room listened until she was through. Then she signed off.

"Good luck, King," she finished. "Remember, take care of yourself."

There had been a little unsteadiness in her voice. The radio went dead. King lighted a cigarette and sat back, crossing his legs.

"I move we go out and have a good look at this yacht," he

ventured. "There's something funny going on. I can't figure it out and I won't be satisfied until I look into it."

"I'll admit there is something strange about a yacht drifting in the Sound without anyone on it," the Bishop said. "You're sure that it is drifting?"

King nodded. "It certainly isn't tied to anything," he said, "and the anchor is up on the forward deck with the rope all coiled nicely in shipshape. But here's the thing that strikes me as the strangest of all. There were two life boats on that craft. One is gone."

"How do you know there were two lifeboats?" the Doctor asked.

"I don't suppose that I do know for certain," he admitted. "But there are two sets of boat arms; one set still holds a boat. In the other, the curbed parts are swung out over the water, and the ropes and tackles are dragging. It looks as though someone deserted the yacht out in the middle of the Sound. Not only that, but deserted the person left on board."

"And left her to drift without throwing the anchor overboard?" the Doctor demanded.

King smiled a little as he nodded. The Bishop was straightening slowly, as though King's last words were dawning upon him.

"Just a minute, gentlemen," he said. "What was that last thing you said, King?"

King's smile broadened.

"I saw you getting it, Bishop," he said. "I said that the man not only deserted the yacht but the other person as well."

The Bishop frowned. "Just what do you mean? How do you

11

know that someone was deserted on board? I thought you just said—"

"I did," smiled King. "I didn't see anyone. But I'm making a pretty good guess that someone was left on board. Someone or his body."

The eyes of the men about him widened.

"His body?" exclaimed the Key. "Hey, listen. You mean there's a stiff on board that yacht?"

King nodded. "I'm just making a guess at that," he said. "You see, I can't figure out any other reason why the flag should be at half-mast."

The Bishop blinked. The Doctor got up.

"Well," he boomed, "what are we all sitting around here for? Let's go and see what there is on board; then we'll know what we're talking about."

"That's my idea exactly," agreed King. "The plane holds six, and I'm pretty sure I can get her out of our little field with capacity load. This is a good time to find out. She's got a pontoon for landing on water, when you lift the wheels. We can fly out to the yacht in a few minutes."

The Doctor shook his head and growled something deep down in his throat.

"If you're figuring me as a passenger in any airplane, you're crazy," he said. "I'll walk before I'll fly."

The Key cut in with, "Listen, I got this all lined up. I ain't been with these thugs most of my life for nothin'. You heard what Flo said just now. They're tryin' to rub you out, King. And that means those mugs, whoever they are, would do anything to kill you."

The Bishop frowned and turned his head to face the Key.

"Do you mean, Key," he said, "that they would place a yacht drifting in the Sound just to lure us out?"

"Mean, hell, I mean, goodness," the Key said. "I'm as sure of it as though these mugs had sent me a post card. You got to admit yourself it's clever. They steal a yacht and put the flag at half-mast and hide in the cabins and let her drift. They don't know where we are but they got a hunch, from what Flo says, that we're somewhere on Long Island. And if their hunch works, we'll come to and see what's phony about the ship—which ain't nothin' I got any idea of tyin' up with."

"I'll pick your locks and open safes and get dope from the panhandlers and stuff like that, and maybe I'll do a little rough stuff sometimes, but when it comes to walkin' right up to a bunch of mugs and spittin' in their faces and tellin' them to try and hit me—uh, uh—count me out. Because Tommy guns don't miss so good."

King laughed.

"Sounds like you're backing out on the party, Key," he suggested.

"You tell 'em I'm backin' out, fella," the Key said earnestly. "I may be able to pick my way out of any jug in this man's world, but when it comes to pickin' the locks on the pearly gates of heaven or the fiery gates of hell, I don't figure it's so good."

King, still smiling, nodded.

"I guess that settles that, then," he said.

He felt a powerful form at his side. It was Luga.

13

"Where you go, Master, Luga go," said the giant black. "But maybe this trap like Key say."

King shrugged.

"That's one of the things we've gotta find out," he said. "How about the rest of you?"

"You can count on me going if you swim, row, walk or take a bus," growled the Doctor. "But if it's flying, that's out. I'm too heavy, anyway, and I like to keep one foot on the ground."

"I HAVE a thought," cut in the Bishop, "that perhaps our cruiser would serve the purpose better than the plan.

"The Doctor will go along in that, I'm sure. Then there is another thing that might be well to consider. Suppose these criminals who seek the life of King are aboard the yacht, waiting for us. If we go by plane and King should be injured, there would be no way of getting him away. But any of us can handle the cruiser."

King nodded.

"Suits me," he said, "if the rest are agreeable."

He glanced at the Key with another grin. The Key shook his head.

"I'll stay and hold the fort or block house or whatever you call this shanty, while the rest of you blockheads go out and hang yourselves," he said. "But if you're going, you'd better take something besides a prayer book because most of the thugs don't even understand that kind of English."

"I think," said the Bishop, "they will understand my gun collection."

He walked to a cabinet and threw open the doors. Rifles and

shot guns gleamed in the light. He took down gun after gun and began handing them about. But King stopped him.

"Maybe two or three rifles will fill the bill for that kind of arms," he suggested. "That Tommy gun that the inventor gave you ought to help a lot. But that drawer of revolvers and automatics will certainly be swell for close work if we do run into trouble."

The Bishop nodded.

"You are right, as usual, King," he said.

He took out the Tommy gun, loaded the cylinder with shells and handed it to King.

"You may have the honor of carrying that ugly weapon," he said. "And Doctor, you and I will carry two high-powered rifles for long range picking if the necessity arises."

He then closed the cabinet and pulled out a drawer beneath it, from which he picked automatics of various makes—Colts, Lugers, etc. These he distributed to Shakespeare and Luga.

King inspected the four who were to accompany him on the trip. The Doctor, the Bishop, Shakespeare and Luga. They were all well-armed and eager to start. He nodded.

"Let's go. Key, you keep the home fires burning."

The Key was serious as he faced his chief.

"Honest, King," he said. "I'd go if I thought there was any use. I wish you'd stay. You'll be the guy that's goin' to burn if my guess about what's on that raft is true. There ought to be some way of findin' out without—"

King patted his slim shoulder.

"Thanks for your worry, Key," he said, "but I've just got a

hunch that everything is going to be okay—as far as I'm concerned. And don't worry about our thinking you're yellow."

Key grinned.

"Thanks," he said.

King led the way out of the cabin. The others trooped behind him. And they made a hard looking crew, those five—King with the Tommy gun and a Luger in his belt, and the rest with various other types of arms.

They reached the Bishop's cruiser and climbed aboard. The engine was started and the boat pushed through the overhanging brush that hid it from the Sound. King was on the bow, scouting for passing boats. Nothing was in sight except that drifting yacht far out.

"All clear," he announced.

The powerful motor rumbled louder and the cruiser shot out into the open.

Minutes passed. The deep, underwater exhaust made little sound. Every eye was strained on the yacht as they approached it.

The yacht was drifting about five miles from the north shore of the island. When they came close enough to see it plainly with the naked eye, they noted the flag still at half-mast. The Bishop stared through binoculars.

"There's a name on her," he said, "but I can't make it out. It's at a bad angle. Wait, I'm getting it. The—the *Parson*. No, that's not it. It's the *PAGAN*. The *Pagan*. Where have I heard of that yacht before?"

He brought down his glasses and frowned as he tried to think.

"The *Pagan*," he repeated. "There's a story connected with it. What is it?"

"She's a splendidly appointed little craft," Shakespeare ventured.

"Wait," said the Bishop. "I've got it. The *Pagan* belongs to one of the Waldorff. Old John Flint Waldorff, if I remember correctly."

They were now so close that the yacht loomed above them.

King was crouched, Tommy gun ready. The Doctor stood on one side of the after cockpit, holding his rifle over the top of the small cabin aimed at the deck of the yacht.

The Bishop picked up his high-powered hunting rifle and aimed it at the same general point of the yacht from the opposite side of the cruiser.

"There's a forward and after entrance to that central cabin," King called back. "You watch both of those. The port holes are open on this side; I'll take care of them."

They were within twenty feet of the larger boat now. So far nothing had happened. Every man on the cruiser was tense, ready for anything.

The Bishop held his rifle ready with one hand and slowed the motor, swinging the cruiser to the east so that they were coming alongside.

King suddenly caught hold of the rail of the yacht. With the Thompson machine gun in one hand, he pulled himself aboard with the other.

"Wait for us," called the Doctor.

But King was already advancing toward the cabin. He moved

in a crouched position, one foot ahead of the other, both hands on the Tommy gun. He could see only the top of the cabin through the windows. Anyone might be hiding below that level, ready to leap up and pour lead into him.

He made a rush for the nearest window, peered down. An exclamation left his lips.

Then, as the Doctor reached him, he died down the few steps into the cabin.

There, in an easy chair, the form of a big, gray-haired man lolled back, arms wide-spread. The mouth gaped open. The eyes were closed.

The Doctor started a hasty examination. But King was staring at the man's throat.

"Jolly," exclaimed the Bishop as he entered. "It's Waldorff. I've never seen his picture but from his description, I don't think I could be wrong."

"Look at his throat," King exclaimed. "It's as black as a black eye."

"He's dead," said the Doctor, straightening.

CHAPTER 3
THE WHITE CANDLE

L UGA HAD leaped into the cabin beside King. A moment later Shakespeare arrived. The five stared down at the corpse. Old John Waldorff was a ghastly sight. His mouth was wide open. His eyes closed and his whole throat was, as King had said, as black as a black eye.

"What is it, Doctor?" King asked. "Was he strangled?"

The Doctor shook his head.

"I wouldn't want to say," he said. "I've examined bodies of men and women who have been strangled. But I never saw a throat like that."

King nodded thoughtfully.

"His face is a natural weather-beaten color. How about fingerprints?"

The Doctor was fumbling in a best pocket with his big powerful fingers. Surprising what minute operations those clumsy looking fingers could perform. He fished out a microscope and began examining the throat of the dead man.

"It looks to me like a perfectly clear case," Shakespeare observed. "John Flint Waldorff was enormously wealthy. He probably carried considerable wealth aboard his yacht and his crew choked him to death when he surprised them in the act of robbery."

He struck a pose with one hand inside his coat.

"John Flint Waldorff passed like all of the great. As Shakespeare said, 'And mighty Caesar turned to clay may stop a hole to keep the wind away.' Ah, yes, gentlemen, is it not so?"

The Doctor seemed to be making a careful examination through his magnifying glass. At length he straightened.

"You're wrong about one thing, Shakespeare," he said. "This man wasn't choked. At least there are no finger marks on his throat."

King frowned. "That is queer. You're sure?"

The Doctor nodded.

"You can see for yourself. Here, let me show you something."

He placed the fingers of both his great hands on King's throat, and pressed until he shut off the wind. Then he relaxed the pressure a bit.

"You can feel my fingers as I press them in on your throat," he said.

"I'll say I can," King choked.

"Now here is what would happen," the Doctor went on, "if I pressed harder. If I pressed hard enough, I would leave bruises. Look at Waldorff's throat. It is uniformly black, not blotched as it would be if fingertips had pressed harder in some places than in others."

King looked at Waldorff's throat as the doctor released his hold.

"You're right," he agreed. "And you say you can't find any fingerprints, either?"

"Not a sign of one," said the Doctor. He handed King the magnifying glass. "Look for yourself."

King did look. He examined every square inch of that blackened throat. He even finished by rubbing the back of his hand across the throat so that none of his fingerprints would be left.

"Expect it to rub off?" asked the Bishop with a twinkle.

"I didn't know," King said. "Thought I'd try, anyway."

"That color is inside," said the Doctor. "It almost looks as though someone had beaten old Waldorff over the throat with a club. But in that case there would be torn skin and broken bones."

"How about the robbery motive Shakespeare mentioned?" King suggested. "Let's have a look about the yacht."

He turned and surveyed the rest of the main cabin. In one corner was a large, double bunk, apparently built especially for the big form of John Flint Waldorff. Chairs were scattered about the room. An expensive radio was lashed to the floor and on top of it stood a queer looking vase.

King picked it up. It was a crude affair about five inches in height and four inches wide at the bottom, from which it tapered up to a small neck. It was empty. Both front and back were covered with strange figures and stranger writings. King looked up at the Doctor, who had joined him.

"What do you make of it? he asked.

The Doctor shrugged.

"A piece of Egyptian pottery taken from a tomb," he guessed.

The Bishop stepped closer to peer at the piece; then he shook his round head.

"I beg to differ with you, but it looks to me more like Mayan sculpture."

"The Mayans were a lost civilization around Yucatan, weren't they?" King inquired.

"Yes," said the Bishop. "In studying for the ministry, we come in contact with Egyptian writing. It isn't anything like this." He turned the vase over and over in his hand and nodded with finality. "Yes, I'm quite positive that this vase is from the lost Mayan civilization.

He returned the piece to the radio cabinet. King frowned at it for a moment, then noticed a wall safe nearby. Wrapping his fingers in a handkerchief so as not to leave fingerprints, he took hold of the door handle. It swung open easily.

"I was right about one thing," Shakespeare exclaimed. "It is evident that the crew were in such a hurry that they didn't bother to lock the safe again."

WHILE HE spoke, King started opening compartments inside. Again he used a handkerchief to shield his fingerprints.

"Wrong again, Shakespeare," he said at last. "If the crew killed Waldorff for money, why didn't they take this?"

He drew out six bundles of bills, each one marked $1,000.

"There's six thousand dollars that somebody missed."

The others stared.

King kept on examining the safe. He found several little gold trinkets of peculiar design, which he showed to the Bishop, who nodded with satisfaction.

"They seem to come from the same general source as that vase," he said. "All of them are Maya, unless I'm greatly mistaken."

"Maya, or perhaps Aztec?" King ventured. "Both races were in the same area of Central America, weren't they?"

The Bishop shook his head.

"Generally so, but the Mayas came first and had a very high type of civilization around the Yucatan peninsula. The Aztecs came from the north and settled farther north around Mexico City, at a much later period. There are plenty of signs yet of the Aztec Indian, but the Mayas are a lost race except for the Indians of Yucatan."

He turned the trinkets over in his hand very slowly.

"Just at a guess," he said, "I'd say that anyone who took these out of the ruins did so at considerable danger to himself. Maya Indians guard some of those ruins rather jealously."

The Doctor spoke up.

"Isn't there a story about the Waldorffs being mixed up with Mayan treasure?" he asked.

The Bishop continued to stare at the gold trinkets thoughtfully.

"Seems to me there was something about it, although I can't recall just what it was," he admitted.

King continued to examine the scant contents of the safe.

There were a few negotiable bond and stock certificates of very high denominations; he added their value rapidly in his mind.

"Phew!" he whistled, "about a half million dollars' worth of stuff in there altogether." He grinned at Shakespeare. "Funny the crew who you think murdered Waldorff didn't take all of this with them. All they had to do was to open the safe and fill a couple of pockets."

"I'm afraid you're right there," Shakespeare said.

King put the valuables back into the safe and glanced about the cabin. Three doors led into it. One, that through which they had entered, came from the forward deck. Another opened onto the after deck. And the third led below.

He opened that third door, found that it brought him into the galley. He scrutinized it carefully. Nothing the least bit out of order there. Dishes were all washed and neatly stacked in their racks.

Closing it, he went up on the forward deck. There in the center of the deck, he noticed a hatch. He lifted it and peered down a steep stairs. For a moment his breath caught in his throat. His eyes had fallen on something strange, very strange. Hurriedly, he climbed down the ladder-like stairs into a small cabin.

It was a very small cabin, with sides tapering where the boat came to a point at the bow. Along one wall was a short bunk. He measured it with his eye. That bunk wasn't six feet in length. No more than five and a half. It was made for a small man to sleep in. It was the only bunk in the cabin, the only one in the whole yacht so far as he knew beside that large, oversized one in the luxuriously appointed stateroom of John Flint Waldorff.

A chair stood across from the bunk. And at the forward end was a small dresser with drawers built in. It was the contents of that dresser top that caused King to stare.

In the exact center stood a vase very similar to the one that was on the radio cabinet top in the main cabin. But this vase had a peculiar looking candle stuck in its small neck.

The candle looked as though it had been molded by small fingers. It was little more than a half inch in diameter at the thickest place and irregular in shape. It was thicker at the top end where the blackened wick stuck out. It had been burned for only a few minutes.

To the right of the candle was a white napkin, which looked as though it were draped over something. And on the very top was a spot of blood.

There was a dirtier white napkin on the other side of the candle. And on top of that, too, was a drop of hardened blood.

Standing against the back of the dresser top was a grotesque little clay figure evidently molded by a rank amateur. A knife blade had cut into the throat of the image and the clay, still fairly soft, was turned outward, gibing that throat a torn look.

King had touched the clay, that was all. He found it slightly pliable. But he reached out to touch other things on the dresser. Then he drew back his hand, glanced behind him.

A door led somewhere from the after end. He opened it on the galley, passed through to the door at the other end of the galley and on opening that, stepped on the lower step of the short stairs that led into the main cabin where the dead man still slumped in his chair.

The cabin was deserted. He called the Doctor and the Bishop, who hurried in from the after deck.

"What's up?" demanded the Doctor.

"What did you find?" King asked in return.

"Nothing," said the Bishop. "There's a cabin under the after deck, but it only houses the engines."

"I've got something I'd like to have you see," King said.

He led them through the galley and into the room with the single short bunk, and pointed to the dresser top.

"What do you make of that?" he asked.

FIRST THE Doctor and the Bishop stared. The three men filled the forward cabin so that they could move with difficulty. The Doctor reached the dresser end first, put his hands out to touch the base and the strangely-shaped candle and the image. Then he drew back and jerked his head toward it.

"That," he said, "isn't Maya, unless I'm crazy."

The Bishop frowned.

"You mean the vase isn't?" he said.

"No, the vase may be Maya, all right. But I mean the whole set-up," the Doctor went on. "That's some form of Black Magic."

King and the Bishop stared at the Doctor blankly.

"You mean," demanded King, "that you think John Flint Waldorff was killed by Black Magic?"

The Doctor shrugged his big shoulders.

"I'm a doctor of medicine and science," he said. "I've never heard of a disease that kills human beings and leaves them with a blackened throat such as Waldorff has. Let's go back into the main cabin and have another look at the body."

As the Doctor turned, King and the Bishop exchanged glances. Was this man trying to tell them he believed in Black Magic?

While the Doctor examined Waldorff's body again in the main cabin, King asked, "Isn't it queer for a man like Waldorff to be running this yacht alone with only one servant? Apparently that's all there were quarters for. And a small servant, at that."

"Not surprising at all," said the Bishop. "After looking at the engine room, I can readily understand it. Waldorff could easily handle the yacht with the twin screw rig he has at the stern."

"How do you account for this, Bishop?" King asked. "That vase in the servant's cabin was almost identical with the vase on the radio here. What's the tie-up?"

"Possibly," said the Bishop, "Waldorff may have picked up his servant on one of his travels about the globe. It may be they got those vases together at the same time."

The Doctor glanced up from the body and smiled.

"I have an idea," he said. "I'd like mighty well to let the police know that they've got some competition in this and other important cases. Suppose I make a mark of The Secret 6 on Waldorff's forehead just to let them know we've been here."

King laughed.

"That would be good," he admitted. "It would be a laugh on the police, who think we're working against them instead of with them. And it would be, perhaps, a little nerve racking to the criminals who might be in on this deal. But a 6 is a 6. How can it be made secret?"

"I'll show you," the Doctor said.

He took from his pocket a stub of an indelible pencil and made a mark on the forehead.

"I'm afraid that I don't see that at all," the Bishop said.

"That must be the secret part of it," grinned King.

"It's very simple," the Doctor told them. "If anyone should want to know, it will be a symbol that The Secret 6 will move the sun and moon to help the down-trodden and stop a crime. But in reality, it's only a number 6 in two parts. Just place the smaller circle in the bottom of the crescent and see what you have."

King did that lightly in the palm of his hand.

"By George," he exploded, "that's right. The Secret 6 sign. A tip to the police that we're in on the case and a warning to the criminals that we're crowding them hard. Swell, Doctor."

The Doctor jerked his head toward the body of Waldorff.

"I'd have to go into this thing a lot deeper if we're going to even make a guess as to what killed Waldorff," he said. "It would take several hours to go into it fully. Either here or—"

A cry from the deck cut off the Bishop's words. It was Luga's deep voice coming to them in hushed tones.

"Master. Ship come this way. Luga think coming to this boat. You come see."

King was up out of the cabin at a bound. He stared across at a dull gray painted craft that was approaching rapidly from the west.

The Bishop appeared behind him. He took one look and an exclamation escaped his lips.

"Jolly, it's a police boat. Quick. Into our cruiser. We may have time to get away, if we hurry."

The police boat was still a good mile away. The five men tumbled into the cruiser that was moored to the starboard side of the drifting yacht, and the Bishop started the engine.

"I believe we're in luck, gentlemen," he beamed. "It happens that our cruiser is moored on the opposite side of the yacht from the police boat. Now, if we can keep the yacht between us and the police boat for a while, we may have a chance."

The cruiser started to the east down the Sound.

"We've got to keep going until everything is cooled off," the Bishop went on, as they gathered speed. "We can't run for home and let the occupants of the police boat see where we are going."

They shot on. The Bishop was steering by looking behind and keeping that yacht between them and the oncoming police boat. Suddenly King, on the after deck, called.

"I think they've seen us! They're swerving in their course to take a good look."

He snatched the Bishop's binoculars and stared through them.

"There's a bird on the forward deck of that police boat watching us through glasses," he said.

The Bishop pushed on the throttle for more speed. But the powerful engine was throbbing with all she had. The police boat was nearing the drifting yacht. It seemed as if it were going to skim past it and keep up the pursuit.

King glanced through the glasses once more.

"An officer is working with the gun on the forward deck," he called.

"We should expect that," said the Bishop. "Even at this distance they can blow us half out of the water with good shooting."

"He's standing by for the order to fire," King called.

"They are putting up the flag that demands our surrender," said the Bishop. "The only thing we can do is ignore it. Everybody down!"

Boom! Wheeeeee! Plunk!

29

There came the dull blast of the bow gun. Then the scream of a shell as it crossed their bow and dropped into the Sound a few hundred feet to the southeast.

CHAPTER 4
BLACK MAGIC

THE BISHOP whirled and measured the distance between the two plowing boats with his narrowed eyes.

"I fear," he said, "that the police will have to shoot and be—er—damned, as the Key would put it."

Suddenly King pointed ahead and to the south.

"Look," he explained. "See that freighter? It's moving east, the same way we're heading."

His finger pointed to a big freighter, less than a mile away, that was plowing the waters of the Sound at a good speed, heading for the cape and the ocean.

"Yes," nodded the Bishop. "I've been thinking of that."

"If we can reach it before the police boat catches up with us, we might be able to duck them on the other side."

"I doubt if we can duck them forever," the Bishop said. "However, we can try. It would take that police boat a good half hour or more to catch us at the rate we're both traveling. If we get out of sight, they may give up the chase."

"Right," said King. "We'll try it."

The cruiser throbbed on, with spray flying from both sides. King stared through the glasses once more.

"Another shot is coming," he called. "Get set. This one will be closer."

"Let her come," yelled the Bishop. "Everybody down."

"Here she comes. I see the smoke from the gun."

Bram! Wheee!

They heard the roar of the gun and at the same time the scream of another shell. This time it splashed into the Sound nearer the cruiser. But even then it missed by a good hundred yards.

"Closer," said the Bishop, "but they've got to come a lot closer before they stop us."

"They will next time," called King. "They shoot one or two wide and then get down to business."

"Yes," said the Bishop. "One to warn and the next to scare and the third comes straight to lay us bare."

King grinned at Shakespeare.

"He's stealing your stuff, Shakespeare," he chuckled, then he swung the glasses again. "That officer on the forward deck by the gun is getting ready to lay us bare right now."

The Bishop nodded. "We'll be ready for them. You watch for smoke. The instant you see it, shout 'turn,' and I'll do the rest. I hope I turn the right way."

King tensed. This shot would mean business. He saw the officer working at the gun, saw him step back, move from a crouched position. Smoke belched from the muzzle.

"Turn," shouted King.

The cruiser swerved to the right.

Boom!

The explosion and the shriek of the shell came to their ears at the same instant. The shell screamed past and plopped to the left, about seventy-five feet away, throwing spray over them as it hit.

"Phew!" whistled King. "That one was close."

"Not as close as it should have been if that gunner could really shoot," the Bishop said merrily. "That shot shouldn't have landed more than twenty-five or thirty feet from us with the turn I made."

"They're getting ready to fire another one," King called.

"And we're almost around this freighter," the Bishop called back. "Hold fast and tell me when you see smoke from the gun again."

"Right," said King. He watched and then an exclamation of joy left his lips.

"They're swerving alongside the *Pagan!* They're stopping there!"

"Great! That will do the trick," boomed the Bishop. "We've almost caught up with the side of the freighter."

As he spoke, the stern of the freighter towered before them. They read the name painted on it.

Knute Hantoon.

"She's Norwegian," the Bishop called. "Wait, I'm going to try something. The police boat won't dare shoot while we're this close to her."

Men were already leaning over the freighters rail.

"Hellooo there," the Bishop called.

One, wearing a captain's uniform, waved, but the stern expression on his face never changed.

"We're police being chased by criminals in one of our own boats," the Bishop went on. "If they ask where we've gone, tell them you don't understand English."

The captain looked perplexed. He shouted to others of his crew, then wagged his head.

"No English," he called back.

"Good," approved the Bishop.

He gave the cruiser full throttle and they shot ahead past the slow-moving freighter.

"I just saw the police boat before we rounded the stern," King told him. "I think they're coming on to finish the chase."

"I think we can beat them," the Bishop said. "There's a small inlet with just water enough for our cruiser. It's way up toward the eastern end of the Island. We'll head for that and keep the freighter between us and the police boat."

They began plowing on past the larger boat, taking a gentle arc toward the shore about two miles ahead where it came out in a point to the north.

"I rather suspected that there wouldn't be anyone on board that Norwegian freighter who could understand English," said the Bishop. "Those police are going to have fun when they try to find out what's become of us."

The Doctor laughed. "That ought to be almost worth waiting for."

The Bishop was again steering the cruiser by looking backward. The freighter was larger and much easier to keep between them and the police boat than the yacht had been.

PRECIOUS MINUTES passed, then they rounded the point of land and turned into a small, shallow bay. The Bishop swung the cruiser around and came back pushing through some trees that overhung the deeper shore. There they stopped and watched.

The police boat rounded the freighter a few moments later. Peering through his binoculars, King watched the police boat pull alongside the freighter. He saw the police officers gesturing.

Saw them getting madder by the minute as they tried to make the captain and his crew understand English.

At length they gave it up and turned away. They made a circle of that end of the Sound, searched the shore line through their glasses. Then they made a wide turn and went back toward the *Pagan*.

King and his men stayed in the hidden inlet until the late afternoon sun settled down in the west at the far end of the Sound. Then, when dusk covered their movements, they pushed out into the deeper waters and made tracks for their jungle hideaway.

The Key, nervous and anxious, met them as they pushed the cruiser into the secret dock.

"Holy gee," he exclaimed," I never expected to see you guys again. Not after I heard that shooting out there."

"You heard it from here, then?" asked the Bishop.

"I'll say I did," the Key grinned. "What did you think I'd be doin' while you birds were out, takin' a nap? And did I kick myself all around the woods for being so yellow that I wouldn't go out with you. But just the same, it looked to me like they had the finger on you this party, King."

King smiled. "I've got to admit I figured about the same thing," he said. "But then we had to find out, and we found plenty. Say—" he turned to the others— "I wonder how the cops got wind of what was going on out there? That was a New York police boat on the Sound, wasn't it?"

"Yes, indeed," said the Bishop. "I can't figure the thing out myself."

King told the Key briefly what they had seen on the yacht. Luga was getting dinner, working over the little oil stove. A fire that Key had kindled was burning merrily in the fireplace. The Key grew nervous as King told him about the dead man with the black throat, but his eyes bulged when King told him about the safe and what it contained.

"Say, listen, King," the Key pleaded. "You don't mean to tell me that these guys would kill somebody and leave a half million dollars in cash and securities in a safe, unlocked, and not help themselves? Phew! What's this world comin' to?"

King smiled tolerantly.

"It certainly looks hopeless sometimes," he said, "doesn't it, Key? Then you'll think I'm pretty dumb to leave the money right there where I found it, I suppose?"

"You mean," the Key shouted, "that you left all that dough there in the safe?"

"It wasn't our money," the Bishop cut in. "You'd better get the right slant on things, Key."

35

"Sure, I know," said the Key, "but listen, Bishop, that dough belonged to the old nut that was murdered. The murderers hadn't taken the dough. And the dough wasn't any use to a dead man, was it? Hell, I mean, goodness, no. And findies is keepsies, ain't they? So what?"

"So we left the five hundred odd thousand dollars' worth of stuff and came home like good boys," King grinned.

The Key groaned, bent over and held his head in his hands.

King turned to the Doctor.

"Well," he asked, "what's your guess about the whole thing? Murder, or was it a disease?"

The Doctor puffed at his cigar. His eyes narrowed.

"A disease?" questioned the Key. "Where do you get that stuff? You find a guy that's been choked so hard that his throat is black and then you think maybe he died of disease."

The Doctor seemed not to hear the Key. He cleared his throat.

"I've been trying to figure the thing out from a disease standpoint," he said. "I never heard of anything like this. There isn't a disease or even a plague known to the medical profession that turns the throat black when the patient dies."

He smoked on. King lighted a cigarette. Then Luga called them all to the evening meal.

Suddenly King stopped short with his fork halfway to his mouth.

"Just what could the hook-up be between the servant in that front cabin and those two similar vases that looked as old as the hills?"

"I believe I can advance a theory on that," said the Bishop.

"Likely the servant could have been with Waldorff when he found those vases. Perhaps there is a story that both of them enjoy together."

King shook his head.

"That isn't just what I mean," he said. "Now, would it be possible for this servant to have been a foreigner that Waldorff had picked up somewhere in his travels?"

"I don't see any connection," the Doctor ventured.

"What I'm trying to do is find some strange disease, say of the Oriental countries, that the medical profession in America know nothing about," King explained.

He went on eating. Turning to the Bishop, he said, "You seem pretty well versed in that sort of stuff, Bishop. Would it be possible for those vases to have been Chinese instead of the very ancient Maya?"

The Bishop considered, then shook his head.

"I'm sure they couldn't be," he said. "There is nothing about them that even hints of the Chinese influence."

"There's one series of facts that seems certain," King said a moment later. "There couldn't have ever been more than one man along with Waldorff on any of his cruises. There were only two bunks on his boat. This servant must have been considered a faithful one of long standing, otherwise the safe would not have been left open."

Suddenly a mumbling sound coming from the short wave receiver gave everyone a start. Words were coming in a dull monotone. There was little or no inflection of words or phrases, and inaudible.

The Key leaped to his feet.

"Pipe down," he hissed. "That's the Dummy speaking. I know him. Maybe he's got dope from the police. He goes there two or three times a day to practice his talkin' with the police surgeon. He can hear a little now and you can tell how much talkin' he can do by listenin' to him now."

The voice came clearer. But the monotonous tone and the slurred phrases could not be picked up any better.

"Cops after you, King. Almost caught Secret 6 boat today. Got all dope—from them just now. Hear me? Don't talk so good. Listen."

EVERY MAN in that room grew rigid. The cabin was still as death. For a long moment no sound came from the speaker of that wave receiver. Then the weird voice of the Dummy began again. It made the chills run up and down King's spine.

"Police think they saw Secret 6 cruiser beside the *Pagan*, owned by John Flint Waldorff. Waldorff's servant, a Mayan Indian named Manaha, came to report that Waldorff was dying. After Waldorff died, Manaha left the yacht in a life boat and rowed all the way back to New York. The cops are holding the Maya for murder. He won't talk except to say he didn't do it. He says Black Magic killed Waldorff."

The voice stopped. Then a moment later the Dummy repeated his message.

"By George," King exploded. "I was going to ask that question about those queer contraptions in the forward cabin—"

The Doctor nodded and lighted a cigar. He seemed to have reached a conclusion.

"That clears that part of it up," he said.

"You mean the funny white gadgets and the candle and things?" King asked.

"Right," said the Doctor.

The Bishop lighted his pipe leisurely.

"If you're trying to say, Doctor," said the Bishop, "that Waldorff was killed by Black Magic, I believe you're a little off. You know, if you think sensibly, this Black Magic we hear about is the—er—bunk as the Key would say."

"Perhaps your books on theology teach you that, Bishop," retorted the Doctor calmly. "But I've lived in the tropics. And I've seen it work. What I can't figure out is what this Maya is doing with Black Magic if he's to blame for the crime."

"Nonsense," snorted the Bishop. "I'm astonished at a man of your intelligence—er—falling for that kind of thing. It seems incredible that one of your standing, Doctor, should be swayed by this superstitious poppycock of sages."

King shot a quick glance at the Doctor. Knowing his quick temper, he expected a flare-up between the two. But he received a shock. The Doctor only settled deeper into his chair, chewed his cigar and smiled.

"I'd give quite a lot, Bishop," he said, "to have had you witness some of the things that I saw in Haiti. And I can assure you that you'd run into a peck of trouble there if you came out flatly and said that Black Magic was bunk."

The Bishop smiled back at him.

"It may be, Doctor," he said, "that my education has been neglected."

"It has," the Doctor assured him.

"You said, Doctor," King reminded him, "that you couldn't figure what a Maya Indian knew about Black Magic. Just what did you mean?"

"This," said the Doctor. "The Mayas know nothing about Black Magic. In fact, I never heard of a Maya Indian who practiced it."

King studied the end of his cigarette for a moment.

"You mentioned both Black and White Magic practiced in Haiti," he said. "Just what is White Magic?"

"They have the two kinds," said the Doctor, "because it's obvious that among those ignorant races there would be argument between their chiefs and voodoo doctors. So when one voodoo doctor begins work to kill someone with Black Magic, another voodoo doctor may, if he suspects the Black Magic, start working in White Magic to counteract that. And White Magic is used by the voodoos to bring dead men back to life to work in the sugar cane fields."

"Jolly," exclaimed the Bishop. "You don't mean to try to convince me, Doctor, that they actually bring men back to life after they've been dead for a long time?"

There came a short nod from the Doctor.

"I wouldn't try to convince you of anything that you didn't want to believe, Bishop," he said. "The only thing I can say is, that I've seen it, as far as any white man has seen it."

"You've seen it?" asked the Bishop.

"Yes, and it's the most horrible sight you can imagine," the Doctor said. "The dead men brought back to life work only at night in the cane fields. No human being could put on that act and make it so realistic. You can smell them a half-mile away. Their skin seems about to drop from their bones. The mold is still on their faces."

The Bishop broke into a laugh.

"Really, Doctor," he said. "You're going a bit too far for a man of your profession."

"I'll have to admit," said the Doctor, wiping the sweat from his brow, "that it was going a little too far for me. I got out of Haiti when things came that close."

"Would it be possible, Doctor," asked King, "that these gadgets we saw on the dresser of the forward cabin could have been intended for a White Magic ritual? They were all white."

The Doctor considered and shrugged.

"It's possible," he said, "but I can't figure it out from that angle. Waldorff was found dead from a cause that a medical man can't fathom."

The Bishop turned to King.

"I hardly think it is fair for me to argue against the Doctor's opinion that Black Magic had something to do with this affair," he said. "Of course, I don't believe it. But on the other hand, none of us can say this is so and that it is not. Our knowledge of the spiritual is very limited. Let us assume then that the Doctor may be right; that Black Magic did kill John Flint Waldorff. Why then, did you ask if these—er—gadgets as you call them, could have been intended for a White Magic ceremony?"

"Simply this," said King. "Because I don't believe that Manaha or whatever the name of the servant is, had anything to do with the death of Waldorff."

"You don't?" said the Bishop and the Doctor together.

King shook his head with finality.

"I can't figure it that way at all," he explained.

THE BISHOP glanced from King to the Doctor and took a long breath. His eyes twinkled as he said, "Jolly, are we all going crazy now?" I rather considered this was a case that was closed before it was opened. The police have the Maya set, holding him for the murder of his master. We have found evidence of Black Magic in the servant's cabin. The police find the same thing, we assume. And the servant admits that his master was killed by Black Magic but he declares he is innocent. It looks like a clear case to me. I have read that tropical people have strange drugs and killing devices."

The Doctor nodded. King nodded in agreement too, but he was smiling.

"All very true and a swell story for the papers, Bishop," he admitted. "But here's something that doesn't fit in that puzzle."

He took a long drag at his cigarette then snuffed it out.

"Did you ever hear of a voodoo practitioner having some thugs plot against the life of a guy like me, for instance, because they're afraid I'm going to cramp the style of their Black Magic?"

He got up from the table, shaking his head.

"That to me," he finished, "is rather strange—and suspicious."

The Doctor, Shakespeare, the Bishop and the Key exchanged significant blank looks. The Key spoke.

"King's got the dope," he said. "I never heard of a thug in

New York gettin' tangled up with one of these voodoo doctors. They'd be too scared. No bulletproof bus would protect them from getting rubbed out at long distance by spirits."

King jerked his head to Shakespeare.

"Let's go, Shakespeare," he said. "Think you can make up my face so that the cops won't know me or suspect make-up at close range?"

Shakespeare rose with dignity.

"Young man," he said to King, "I can make you up so that you could kiss your maiden aunt and give her a thrill, so to speak."

"S—uc—stuc," clucked the Key. "Shakespeare, I'm surprised. You'll have to lay off me, Bishop, and give Shakespeare a helping hand. The morals of this outfit is going all to—"

"Ah—ah—ah," cut in the Bishop with a twinkle.

Then the Bishop turned to King.

"Just where do you think you're going?" he asked. "Did I hear you say something about the police?"

"Right," said King. "I'm going to get the Dummy to tell me where Manaha is jailed. Then I'm going to interview him as a press correspondent or something. I'll figure that out later.

"My Go—," the Key began.

"Ah—ah—ah," the Bishop cut in.

The Key grinned. "Fooled you that time, Bishop," he chuckled. "I was goin' to say, my goodness anyway. You mean, King, you're goin' down there to the police and have a rag chewin' contest with the Indian?"

"That's what I aim to do," King said. "Come on, Shakespeare.

43

Let's get busy. Make my face look like someone else's besides mine. I don't care much whose."

He reclined in an easy chair while Shakespeare worked on him.

"You will have to have a press card to see the Indian," the Bishop warned. "I haven't the slightest idea how you are going to manage that end of it."

King kept his face straight while Shakespeare worked.

"Neither have I right now," he said. "I've got some other places to go first. Then I'll see how the press card works out. I want to talk with the Dummy and Flo the Fleecer and then I'll be ready to go to the station."

The Key grinned. "So you're goin' to have a date with Flo," he said. "I wondered how long it would be before you'd be fallin'. Well, she's a swell lookin' jane and a good guy. Don't blame you."

"This happens to be a business call, Key," King said.

Shakespeare worked on. Then when he was finished, King looked at himself in the mirror.

"Not bad at all, Shakespeare," he said. "I sure don't look any more like myself than you do."

"And those fingerprint changes will keep you out of plenty of trouble," the Doctor reminded him.

Luga stepped up and bowed.

"Luga go with you, Master?" It was a question.

King smiled as he shook his head.

"Thanks, Luga," he said, "but this is a job I've got to do alone. I don't think you'd enjoy it much, anyway. There won't be any lighting if my guess is correct."

King changed his clothes to a good suit and started toward the door. On the threshold he turned back to face the other members of The Secret 6 band.

"If need help, I'll try to get word through over the short wave radio," he said. "Good night. Sit tight until I get back or until you hear from me."

Luga followed him out. Walked with him to the place where the light sedan and the big roadster belonging to the band were hidden.

King hesitated as he passed the narrow, long field that was to be their private airport from then on. He feasted fond eyes on the new plane he had bought that morning.

"I'd like to go everywhere in her," he said, "but I guess it's better if I take the roadster tonight. It's getting toward evening and I've got some time to kill and some thinking to do before I reach the police station."

He climbed into the roadster and started the powerful engine. Luga leaned against the door with a sad look on his great black face.

"You be careful, Master," he begged. "You want help, you send word. Luga come quick."

King patted his giant arm.

"I know you will, big boy," he said. "Good night and take care of the rest of the gang."

Then he backed the car out of hiding, turned onto the bedrock drive that left no tire marks and headed for the main highway along the north shore of Long Island.

CHAPTER 5
MANAHA

IT WAS DARK by the time King swung over the bridge into the Bronx and turned downtown. He stopped at an uptown drug store to telephone Flo, the Fleecer.

Her musical voice came rippling across the wires in reply.

"Flo, this is King."

"Well," the girl exclaimed, "this—certainly—is a—pleasure. I never dreamed you'd call me, King."

"I'd like to see you for just a minute, on my way downtown," King said. "About that report you shot out this morning, you know."

"Oh," said Flo. "Oh, yes. Of course. I'll be looking for you."

King noted a little catch in the girl's voice.

"Thanks," he said. "Be right down."

Back in the roadster again. Then he was pulling up in front of the luxurious apartment where Flo lived. She was waiting for him in the ninth floor hall when the elevator stopped.

"You've never been up here before," she said. "I thought I'd better come out of my den and show you the way."

King smiled and bowed.

"That's good of you, Flo," he said.

They entered Flo's apartment. It was simply furnished. Nothing gaudy about the place and still an air of luxury and complete comfort.

They lighted cigarettes.

The light in the hall had been very dim. Now that Flo saw him in a brighter light, she gave a little start.

"What's happened to your face, King?" she inquired.

King laughed. "I didn't think you'd recognize me out there except that I walked toward you in the dim light," he said. "You see, I'm a newspaper reporter for tonight. That is, if I can get a press card."

He told Flo then what had happened during that day. Her beautiful eyes widened as she listened and never left his made-up face. She was particularly charming this evening. Ruffles of white organdy fluffed about her white throat and shoulders.

"I wish I could help you with a press card," she said. "But I'm afraid—now let's see."

King laughed. "You wouldn't know any reporters well enough to borrow their press card," he said. "They don't make money enough."

She didn't get angry, but simply smiled back rather wistfully.

"I'm afraid that's too true," she said. "But seems to me there was an editor a year or so ago. Now let me see."

"Forget it," King said. "What I came to see you about, Flo, was the men you overheard in the night club last night. Were they foreigners or Americans? What did they look like? Do you know who they were?"

"Oh, those," Flo said. "I'll tell you all about it. We were seated at a table in a quiet corner. In fact we had rather a secluded table with curtains hung on either side of us but open at the front. I heard these two men talking through the curtain behind us.

"I heard them mention you, King, but no mention of anyone

who might be hiring them, although I'm sure that someone is hiring them to do the job.

"The one with a deep voice was telling the other who spoke with an Italian accent, that you were to be killed. Those weren't the exact words, of course. The Italian wanted to know where to find you. The deeper voice said that you were with your Secret 6 somewhere on Long Island. He said he'd find out more about it and let the Italian know as soon as he got his assistants rounded up.

"When we danced, I passed very close to their table and got a good look at them. I recognized the one with the deep voice. He's a small politician named Krano. I think he's Italian by parentage, too, for that matter. Although he gets a lot of things done, he always stays on the safe side."

"In other words," King said, "this Krano has contact with the underworld so that he knows who to hire for certain kinds of jobs. Is that it?"

"Yes," said Flo. "No doubt he has been hired by someone much higher up to do away with you. I heard him say that you had to be out of the way so that another job could be pushed ahead more easily."

King smiled. "I'm certainly flattered," he said.

"You've earned it," she tossed back at him. "And I found out roughly who the other one is. I couldn't get his name but he's leader of a small killer gang that commit murders for a living. They used to be on some of the smaller rackets and bootlegging jobs but now that isn't so profitable. Killing is the thing now."

Both men tumbled to the sidewalk.

"Lovely," nodded King, rising. "I've got to get underway again. Thanks, Flo. Keep in touch with us, won't you?"

"Indeed I will, King," she promised. "And please do take care of yourself. The police might suspect you and if they did—"

"They wouldn't get far with fingerprints," King said at the door of the apartment. "The Doctor has fixed that."

"Good," said Flo, beaming. "But don't forget your danger with these killers. Oh, I almost forgot to tell you. I saw Krano with your picture taken from the paper when you were framed for murder on that last case. It was a good enough picture of you so that they would recognize you from it. In fact, I have one of those pictures here myself."

King grinned. "Collecting a rogue's gallery of your own?" he asked.

"Umhum," she smiled back. "And I've started with the nicest rogue I know. Good night and good luck, King."

They parted at the elevator. King went straight to his roadster outside and drove downtown to the haunt of the Dummy. He parked the car just past the corner where the Dummy usually stood with his blank, sightless eyes, his tin cup and his cane.

He got out and walked around to the Dummy. He waited for some time to make sure that the Dummy wasn't being watched. Then King approached him.

THE DUMMY was a pitiful sight. His lips seemed to move constantly though no sound came from them, only an almost inaudible monotone of moaning. That was mostly for affect, to make the passers-by feel sorry for him.

Now and then passers-by stopped to drop coins in his tin cup.

King took him by the arm. The Dummy turned his head as though he were looking at King, who moved him a half-step.

He put his lips close to the Dummy's right ear.

"The Key," he said loud enough for a slightly deaf person to hear.

There came the slightest nod of the Dummy's head. Then he came willingly. They walked around to King's car and got in. So far as King could notice, no one had watched or followed them. King pushed the Dummy into the car gently and helped him settle into the seat. Then he slipped behind the wheel and the roadster moved off.

As they got out of that district, King put his lips close to the Dummy's ear again and said, "I'm King. I want to go to the police station where they have the Indian servant of Waldorff. What jail is he in?"

The Dummy spoke now in that weird, singsong voice of his. "The Maya Indian servant was held in a midtown police station jail back of the office."

"Okay. Thanks lots," said King. He finished his circle of the block and came back to his first parking-place. He got out and led the Dummy back to the place he had met him, then went back to the car.

King drove past the station and parked halfway down the block. Then he got out and walked back to jail.

For some time he hung about the outside of that sub-police station. He saw a stoop-shouldered, medium built man in plain clothes go in. King saw he was just under middle age. The man nodded to a police officer who was coming out of the place at that moment, and stopped him.

"Hey, listen," the man in plain clothes asked, "what's the chances on gettin' the story about Waldorff and his wooden Indian?"

The cop shrugged.

"Not much, I guess. They're keepin' it pretty close. See the captain and show him your press card. Maybe he'll let you in from the *Gazette*. He isn't takin' any tabloid stuff."

The man in plain clothes went in. The cop came out and, passing King, walked down the street swinging his club jauntily.

King walked up the steps and stood near enough to the entrance to hear what went on inside. He could see the reporter from the *Gazette* standing in front of a desk. A police captain behind the desk was telling him, "There'll be no talkin' to the wooden Indian tonight so you might as well go down to your editor and tell him nothin' doin'."

"Say, listen, captain," the reporter pleaded. "I'll lose my job if I don't get that story. No kiddin'. I got to talk to that wooden Indian that was flunky to Waldorff. Why, this is the biggest story that's busted open in the old town since—"

He stopped short.

"Yeah, go on," snapped the captain. "Say it. The biggest job since that Red Shadow case a while ago. And after the ride you guys took us police with that Secret 6 outfit havin' the laugh on us, you expect us to welcome you with open arms when this real story comes on?"

"But listen, captain," pleaded the reporter. "I didn't have—"

"Oh," snapped the captain, "so you wasn't on the job. You was on your vacation, I suppose. Come on now. Get going. Clear out because we got business. Go peddle your papers and don't be hangin' around here to—"

"But captain—"

"Get goin'—" boomed the voice of the captain.

King ducked from the outside of the doorway as he saw the reporter turn dejectedly and start for the street. King's brain was working like mad. He must have a press card. And he must think of some way to put himself over as a more important reporter than this one seemed to be.

Suddenly he stopped short, snapped his fingers.

"Got it," he said to himself.

He had seen the reporter slip his press card into his right-hand outside coat pocket. That pocket must be picked. The reporter could get another one.

King leaped down the steps and trotted down the street. Then he turned in front of the second house down and came tearing at top speed for the steps of the police sub-station again. He was timing it perfectly. The reporter was coming down the steps.

King was dashing at top speed. With the course he was holding, he would miss the reporter by a scant margin.

But as he swerved, he pretended to stumble. He crashed headlong into the reporter. Both men went down on the sidewalk. King turned his shoulder and turned as he fell, breaking both his fall and the fall of the innocent reporter so that he couldn't be hurt.

And during that fall and the struggle to get up and become

untangled, King's hand slipped into the pocket of the reporters coat.

His hand came out with the press card and, slipping it into his own pocket, he sputtered apologies.

"Awful sorry, old man. I stumbled or maybe my foot hit a banana peel. Boy, what a spill. Wonder we didn't both break our necks. Here, let me brush you off. Mighty sorry."

The reporter grumbled something about looking where he was going, as he was brushed off and half turned.

"Hey," he said suddenly, "where were you going? Police headquarters? What's up—a murder or a fire or something?"

King hesitated for a split second. He was still panting a little.

"I just started working for the *Globe* tonight as a reporter," he panted. "They sent me down to find out about this Waldorff—"

That was as far as he got. The reporter from the *Gazette* grinned.

"Don't let 'em kid yuh," he said. "You can't get anything out of this gang. They're just as mum as that wooden Indian that they got in the jail back of the office. Won't nobody talk."

King straightened. Tried to act the eager young reporter who was going to get his story or die.

"I'll get the story," he panted. "This is my first assignment and I've got to get a good story to hold my job."

AT THAT point a police officer came to the door to see what was going on. King turned and started up the steps. He heard the *Gazette* reporter laugh and start on down the street.

The police officer stopped him at the door.

"Well, what do you want?" the cop demanded.

"I'm a reporter—" King lowered his voice—"on the *Gazette*," he said. "I've got to get this story."

"Well, for the love of Mike," the cop said, "didn't that guy tell you, you couldn't get it. He's from the *Gazette*, too."

"I know, but I know some things that he doesn't know about the case," King said, acting the part now of a very wise, cocksure reporter. "And I got five bucks in my jeans that says after I whisper in the captain's ear, I'll even talk to the wooden Indian."

"Five bucks, says you," chuckled the cop. "I'll take that little bet, son, and you better have the dough ready because I'll be right here waitin' at the door to collect."

"Swell," grinned King, not too sure of himself.

He barged past the cop at the door and walked rapidly up to the desk of the captain. The captain glared at him. King flashed his press card with that same grin still frozen on his face.

"*Gazette* reporter," he said. "I came to get the story about Waldorff and talk to the Maya Indian servant."

The captain's face reddened.

"Say, look here," he bellowed," what is this gettin' to be, a game? Hey, a couple of you fellows, throw him out on his ear. I've had enough of these *Gazette* reporters for the last five minutes. Get out and go back and tell your boss that there ain't goin' to be any story until we get what we want. You fellas think you can ride us all over the yellow sheets whenever you want to. I'll—"

At his command, two husky cops had risen from benches and were coming toward King. One loomed on either side of him. King stood his ground and only grinned.

"Maybe if you'll listen to the story I got for my paper already on this, you'll see it's different," he suggested.

The captain's eyes widened.

"Huh? Hey, what you talkin' about? What's the story you got about this Waldorff case?"

"Lean your head over the desk and I'll whisper it in your ear, captain," he chuckled.

The captain hesitated. His face grew redder. Then he leaned.

King put his mouth close to the captain's ear and whispered in a stage whisper so that almost every cop in the room could hear.

"You're scared that the papers are going to learn the fact that The Secret 6 are giving you a run for your money on this job.

The face of the captain turned purple.

"Who the devil says so?" he roared.

"I did," grinned King. "And I got all the dope. One word from me and the whole story to date goes to press—"

The captain simply stared and blinked. Then he said:

"I think you're a cockeyed liar."

King shrugged and turned.

"Okay, captain," he grinned. "You're the boss. But don't be surprised if you see the picture of old John Flint Waldorff in the *Gazette* tomorrow morning with the mark of The Secret 6 on his forehead."

He had taken two steps toward the door as he said that. But a bellowing roar from the captain stopped him.

"Hey, come back here, young fella," the captain called. "Hey, you, Monahan, at the door. Stop that young idiot."

King turned with apparent reluctance.

"Did you call me, captain," he asked with maddening calm.

"I'll say I called you. Now tell me, how did you know so much? There hasn't been anybody seen Waldorff's body but us and the police surgeon. The body is down at the morgue with a row of police around it two feet thick. And nobody's goin' to see that body until we get good and ready to let 'em, either."

"Nobody but me," King said. "You see, I'm going to have a little talk with Manaha, Waldorff's servant. Then I'm going down to the morgue and take a look at Waldorff's body. And you're going to give me a pass to get by the cops. That is, you are unless you want my paper to get hold of the fact that The Secret 6 is in on this job. And you know what that'll mean. The whole town'll have a better laugh than any comedian has raised since Weber and Fields—or maybe since that Red Shadow case."

The face of the police captain went white. His great fists opened and closed convulsively for a moment.

"And you reporters talk about losing your jobs," he said. "What do you think happens to the police when a bunch of jail-breakers like The Secret 6 makes fools out of us?"

King had to admit to himself that he did feel sorry for the police captain. But he hid that feeling because he had work of his own to do.

"Looks to me as though it's up to every one of us to hold our own jobs," he said. "Do I get that conference with Manaha?"

The captain looked for a moment as though he were going to blow up. Then he nodded to one of the cops.

"All right," he said. "Take this damned reporter and let him talk to the Indian. Not that it'll do him any good. We got a clear case against him."

Then the captain swung back and faced King.

"But remember your agreement," he said. "If I let this go through, you don't say a word to your paper or any other paper about The Secret 6 being on this job."

"Right," said King. "And now about that written pass so I can get by your guard at the morgue."

The captain nodded, scrawled on a slip of paper and handed it to King.

"Has anyone seen the body since it was taken to the morgue? King asked.

"Only members of the family to identify it," the captain said.

"I understand you found the body on Waldorff's yacht," King went on. "Did you notice anything strange about it?"

The captain shrugged.

"Plenty," he said. "The Indian rowed in to tell us Waldorff was dead. We held him here while we went out. It's a clear case against him all right. He murdered the old man by choking him. The surgeon says it's the worst case of choking he's ever seen or heard of. Said this Indian must have choked him so hard that his throat turned black. The safe was rifled of everything. Waldorff's family say he used to carry large sums of money and securities in that safe."

King tensed. "And the safe was empty, is that it, captain?"

"Right," said the captain.

King had all he could do to hide his surprise. The cop led him through a door in the back of the office and down a corridor flanked on either side with cells. They stopped in front of one and a swarthy little man peered calmly at them through the bars.

CHAPTER 6
"STOP THAT MAN!"

THE COP who had conducted him thus far, jerked his head toward the little man behind the bars.

"Well," he rasped. "There he is. Go ahead and talk."

King nodded. "Alone, if you don't mind."

The cop scowled and turned.

"All right," he said. "I suppose we got to give you what you want. But I'll be back before long."

He turned and left the way they had come. King waited until he had closed the door to the office. Then he faced the under-sized Maya Indian.

"You talk English?" he asked.

The Indian nodded, with the slightest change of expression on his face.

"Talk good English," he said.

"Then we're going to get along swell," King said. "First I want to tell you this. You're in a tight spot. And I'm here to figure some way of getting you out."

Manaha glanced at him suspiciously.

"You want me to talk. You not care whether I get out."

King shook his head.

"That's not the idea at all," he said. "You think I'm a newspaper reporter."

Manaha nodded. King lowered his voice.

"I'm not," he hissed through the bars. "I'm here to help you get out of this mess. If you'll tell me the truth, it will help a lot."

"What you want to know?"

"The whole story as it happened," King said.

The Indian thought for a moment, then shook his head.

"Manaha not kill Mr. Waldorff," he said. "Maya curse kill him."

"All right," said King. "Let's start there. What makes you think that the Maya curse killed Waldorff? From what I've heard, you said Black Magic killed him. How come you change?"

The Indian seemed perplexed.

"Maybe both same thing," he said finally. "Manaha not know. First Manaha think Black Magic kill Mr. Waldorff. He get sick fast. Manaha know he be threatened by curse of Maya. Always 'fraid of Maya curse, Mr. Waldorff. But he get sick and Manaha think maybe Black Magic. So Manaha start with White Magic. It not work. Mr. Waldorff die. Now Manaha think maybe not Black Magic."

"I see," said King, "and you think that because the White Magic show you put on didn't save Waldorff that it couldn't have been Black Magic. Is that it?"

Manaha nodded.

"Yes. Maybe it only Maya curse."

"Only Maya curse," King exploded.

Manaha nodded. "Yes. Maya curse not come often. Only come to people that rob temples of my ancestors. Not often then."

"I see," said King. "Then this Maya curse is rare?"

"Yes, Mr. Waldorff say most of his family afraid of Maya curse. He say he not afraid. Not believe."

King shook his head with a baffled look.

"Manaha," he said, "I'm afraid I'm getting more and more in the fog. Suppose you tell me just why the Waldorffs should be cursed by Maya."

The Indian hesitated for a long moment. His dark eyes were studying King's face. Then he spoke.

"Manaha not know much," he said. "Waldorff family have much money. Manaha hear they get this money from Maya ruins. Years ago."

King's eyes widened.

"So that's it. Now we're getting somewhere. The Waldorffs, in years past, opened some Mayan temples and were cursed by the gods. How did you happen to meet John Flint Waldorff?"

"Mr. Waldorff come to Yucatan thirty years ago," said Manaha. "He lone man. Like travel. Got plenty money. He want to see the Maya temples his father tell about."

"Did he come alone?" King asked.

"Yes. He hire me for guide. We dig in ruins. Not find much. Few little gold trinkets in one place. Vases in another."

"Then Mr. Waldorff kept you on as his servant. Is that it, Manaha?" King asked.

"Yes."

"Are those two vases on his yacht from that excavating expedition?" King inquired.

"Two vases, yes. They oldest we find. Down in under temple.

One temple under another. We keep, each have one. Mr. Waldorff good man. He tell me he give me half of everything that we find."

"That was damned decent of him, wasn't it," King said.

He thought for a moment. The tread of feet sounded from the other end of the corridor; a moment later the policeman who had escorted him to the cell came into view.

"Say, ain't you been talkin' to this Indian long enough to get the dope you want for your paper?" he demanded.

"Just about," King grinned. "Come back in another few minutes."

The cop shrugged, then with an air of resignation, he returned and closed the door at the end of the cell block.

KING TURNED to Manaha. "About this voodoo or Black Magic business. How did you become interested in it?"

The black eyes of the little Indian studied him carefully once more. He seemed satisfied. Went on.

"We go to Haiti. Mr. Waldorff hear about Black and White Magic. He give me money, learn how to be voodoo doctor."

King shook his head.

"Boy, I'll say he didn't have much to occupy his mind if he took up voodoo for a pastime," he chuckled. "You say he gave you money to study voodoo?"

"Yes."

"And you learned to kill people at long range without their knowing about it. Is that it?"

Manaha shook his head.

"Manaha learn White Magic," he corrected. "Mr. Waldorff

say maybe Maya curse come back. Then maybe if I learn White Magic, Manaha can drive curse away."

King nodded.

"It looks as though Mr. Waldorff rather thought he might get the curse. Do you know what made him fear this curse?"

"Mr. Waldorff tell me once he think maybe his father die of Maya curse," the Indian answered.

"His father died of the curse," King exclaimed. "Well, that is something. What connection did his father have with the treasure the Waldorffs got from the Maya temples?"

But the Indian only shrugged.

"Not tell Manaha," he said.

"Do you know any of the other members of the Waldorff family?" King asked.

To his surprise the Indian shrugged again.

"Never see any member of family but Mr. Waldorff."

"You mean he never took you along when he visited them?" King demanded. "He did get off his yacht sometimes, didn't he?"

"Sometimes we land New York like just now. Manaha go get provisions. Not know where Mr. Waldorff go."

"Did he say anything about his family?" King asked.

"Once he tell me brother die. He go to New York to funeral."

"How long ago?"

"Two months ago. Mr. Waldorff very sad. Sit long time, look out window for days. Manaha believe he try to figure something out."

King's brain spun a little at that.

"Say," he said suddenly, "how did his brother die? Do you know?"

"Manaha never ask Mr. Waldorff question," said the Indian. "He tell me after funeral he either die of Maya curse or somebody choke him."

"What?" shouted King.

"Not know for sure but think he die maybe like Mr. Waldorff."

"With a black throat?" King demanded.

The Indian nodded.

"Boy, we are getting somewhere now," King exploded in a low voice. "So Mr. Waldorff's brother died in the same way. Look here. Why did you put that flag at half-mast before you left the yacht?"

He scrutinized the Indian's facial expression closely. But there was no look of surprise or suspicion on it.

"Manaha know Mr. Waldorff get very sick. Not have pain. He just get weaker. Manaha try to work White Magic. Then I come back in his cabin. Find him dead. Manaha see flag at half-mast when man dies. Think that help to make white man's God feel good, so put flag at half-mast and take boat and row. Not know how to make yacht go. Come to New York and tell police Mr. Waldorff dead."

"And did you know, Manaha," King hurried on, "that the safe in Mr. Waldorff's cabin contained a large amount of money?"

"When we leave New York, safe have thousand dollars in bills and some papers."

"How did you know that?" King demanded.

The Indian's eyes widened in surprise.

"Mr. Waldorff tell me combination of safe when we get yacht. Manaha always take money from it to buy provisions."

"Did you know that when I examined that safe," King said, "the door was unlocked?"

The Indian's mouth dropped open.

"Manaha sorry," said the Indian in all sincerity. "Manaha forget to lock it, maybe."

"And did you know," King went on, "that the captain of police just told me that when they came aboard the yacht, the safe had been emptied?"

The Indian stared at him.

"Manaha not take money."

"I know," said King, "but when they get you in court, they're going to probe you did. They're going to probe that you killed Waldorff and then took the money."

The Maya shook his head.

"They cannot probe what is not so."

"No," said King. "Maybe not, but you don't know these American courts. I know that you didn't take the money because I was there and saw the money and securities in the safe. I took them out and put them back. Then the police boat arrived. There was no one on board between the time we left and the arrival of the police."

"Maybe police take money," ventured the Indian.

"Maybe," said King, "but I don't like to think so. Something mighty queer happened in that short space of time and I'm going to find out what it is."

He turned and started down the corridor as the cop who had led him in put in his appearance once more.

"Don't worry and just tell the story as you told me as often as you have to, Manaha," he advised. "Don't let them wear you down to anything but the truth."

HE STRODE past the officer and into the office. Went around to the front of the captain's desk.

"Captain," he said. "Was anyone with you beside the police when you went to investigate the *Pagan?*"

The captain blinked and stared hard at him.

"Sure," said the captain. "We took the Indian along to show us where the yacht was."

"Anybody else?" King demanded.

The captain stared harder at him.

"Say, look here," he bellowed. "You're takin' too much in your own hands. Anybody would think you was givin' me the third degree before sendin' me up to the grand jury."

King grinned.

"No offense, captain," he said. "I only asked a simple question. If I can solve this, I'll be glad to give you the credit if you'll lend me a hand in working it out. Was anybody else with you beside the Indian and the police?"

The captain opened his mouth to speak. Then he left it open. A scuffling sound of running feet came from the street door. King turned and his blood ran cold for a second.

The reporter on the *Gazette* was tearing into the room. He was pointing his finger at King, shouting as he came.

"That's the guy," he yelled. "He bumped into me and knocked

me down. I never saw him on a newspaper in my life. He hooked my press card out of my pocket. I'll gamble five bucks to a plug nickel he's got it on him now."

King began thinking with lightning speed. He must not act nervous or guilty. A thought came to him and he hailed the cop who had been standing by the door—the one with whom he had bet five dollars a short time before.

"Hey," he shouted," how about that five bucks you owe me? I got past the captain and the Indian and got the story. Come on. Fork over."

For a split second, that switched attention from the angry reporter to the policeman at the door.

But King was working fast in that split second. The press card was neatly tucked away in his outside right coat pocket. He also carried his box of matches there.

His right hand crept to that pocket. He managed to get the box open and drew out a match. The cop at the door was sauntering dejectedly into the room.

"I don't know about that," he said. "You got in all right, but if you got in under false pretenses, maybe that bet wouldn't hold."

King fought to strike the match with one hand. It was a trick not easily done, especially in all the excitement. But he made it. He felt the match flame, struck it against the tips of the other matches. His fingertips blistered as the box caught. Quickly he shoved the card next to the matches that were now burning his pocket.

CHAPTER 7
A CORPSE WALKS

"FIRE! FIRE!" King's shout for help brought the call from others. Police rushed him from all sides. The side of his coat was blazing. King was putting on a good show, acting like a madman as though the fire had made him forget all he knew about the proper thing to do to extinguish it.

The whole side of his coat was smoldering and blazing now. It felt uncomfortable under his arm pit, but he knew if he could keep it going an instant longer, the press card would be burned and the ashes crushed.

Then a cop dashed at him with an overcoat, which he threw over the smoldering cloth. The cop was a powerful fellow and he seized King in a great bear hug and held on until the overcoat smothered the fire.

King relaxed. The cop let go and took the big coat away. King looked down ruefully at the charred side of his suit coat. Not only the match box and press card had vanished, but the entire pocket, plus a good share of the side of his coat was burned away.

Here and there some smoldering sparks still burned. He and the cop brushed those out with their hands.

"Hey, how about my press card," piped the *Gazette* reporter. "Search him. He's got it on him. I'd bet—"

At that moment, at the mention of a bet, King noticed that the big cop who had smothered his flaming coat was the one with whom he had made the five dollar wager.

"Say," he cut in. "Speaking of bets. You're the cop that owes me five bucks. Well, I guess you did five bucks worth of good in putting me out. We'll call that bet off if it's okay with you, officer."

The cop grinned and nodded.

"Now there's a game sport, boys."

"Hey, search that guy for my press card," yelled the reporter. "He ain't any reporter. He—"

The big cop that had just saved five dollars turned on the *Gazette* man.

"All right," he flared. "Go ahead and search him yourself. But don't be throwin' any threats about who is what and which isn't."

The reporter advanced gingerly. King grinned back and held his arms outstretched.

"Sure," he said. "Go ahead and search me if you like."

The reporter was going through his pockets. He finished and stared blankly at King.

"What did you do with that press card?" he demanded.

King laughed. "If I were you," he said, "I wouldn't want to look any more foolish than I had to. Just because I get a story you couldn't get to first base with, you accuse me of not being a reporter. Boy, if I'm not a reporter, I don't know what they'd call you, fella."

The captain bellowed from behind his desk. Bellowed at the *Gazette* man.

"You know where you stand now," he said. "Get out and stay out."

The reporter turned dejectedly toward the door. King, watching, felt sorry for him. But there was nothing he could do right now. Nothing except to tell him the story he had promised the captain not to repeat to any newspaper.

He waited until the reporter had gone down the steps and disappeared. He wanted to repeat the question he had been asking when the newspaperman had interrupted. But he'd come plenty close to being caught. There was a way out now. And he had a pass to the morgue in his left-hand pocket.

He turned nonchalantly to the captain.

"Thanks for your cooperation, captain," he said. "If I get any dope, I'll see what I can do. Good-night."

"Good-night!" bellowed the captain in a tone of voice that indicated the sub-station head was mighty glad to get rid of him.

He went out to the sidewalk and walked down the block. At the corner he turned, found his parked roadster and slid in behind the wheel.

Five minutes later the roadster drew up before the morgue. He stepped out importantly and walked straight for the entrance. Several police officers were standing just inside the door. Two of those stepped up to him; the others formed a half circle, barring his entrance to the inner part of the morgue.

"Hey, where do you think you're goin'?" the biggest of the two demanded.

King grinned at him. Jerked his head toward the inner rooms of the morgue.

"Who, me?" he said. "I'm goin' in to see the body of John Flint Waldorff."

"Oh, yeah?" came back from the big cop. "And who do you think is goin' to help you get in?"

KING REACHED in his pocket and flashed the piece of paper with the scrawled writing on it that the captain of the sub-station had given him.

"The captain's a friend of mine," he grinned. "That make you feel better about it?"

The big cop looked at the note. His eyes widened.

"Well I'll be—say for the love of Mike, boys, listen to this. We get sent over here by the captain with orders not to let the devil himself into the morgue to see that body. And now comes this wise reporter with orders from the captain to let him do anything he wants. I suppose that means you can put the body over your shoulder and walk out of the place with it, eh?"

King laughed.

"It won't be quite that bad," he said. "John Flint Waldorff isn't any pygmy. If I want to carry him out, I'll call on a couple of you huskies to help."

"Well of all the nerve," exploded the cop. "And who do you think you are givin' orders around here?"

Then something devilish seized hold of King. His made-up face sobered with mock gravity.

"I wouldn't fool you brave men," he said. "I'm King of The Secret 6."

It had seemed a good joke up to the time that those words left his lips. Then he realized what he had said. He tensed inwardly as he watched the facial expressions of those police officers.

"Oh, yeah?" one boomed. "And I'm the Prince of Wales and I got George Washington and Napoleon and all the gang with me. Listen, fella, if you're as nutty as you sound, you belong in a bug house."

"I got a good start here in the morgue," King laughed. "This whole thing looks nutty to me. Tell me this. How many of the family have been down here to identify the body of Waldorff?"

The officer produced a note book and opened it.

"I'm thinkin' that just about all the family was here," he said. "There was old Henry Waldorff. He did most of the talkin'. And there was his son, George, and there was Miss Connie. Now there's a girl for yuh. Mighty bright girl, and pretty as a picture."

"Who's daughter was she?" King asked.

"She's the daughter of James Waldorff that died a couple of months ago," the policeman answered.

"You mean John Flint Waldorff's brother who died from the Maya curse?" King asked.

The eyes of the big cop narrowed.

"Who the devil said he died of a curse?" he demanded. "So help me I'll be puttin' you in the bug house before long. James Waldorff died because a burglar choked him so hard that he left his throat black and blue."

King nodded.

"I see," he said. "Just like some other burglar came aboard John Flint Waldorff's yacht and choked him until his throat was black and blue. Is that it?"

"It was no burglar that came aboard and choked old John Flint Waldorff," the officer flared with certainty. "Sure and it was that dark-skinned, slinkin' Indian servant of his that done it.

A figure sat on that marble slab—it was the dead man!

"Okay," said King patiently. "Now one more question. How long ago was it that the body was examined?"

"You mean by the police surgeon?"

"Yes."

"About four hours ago," came the answer.

"Okay," said King. "Now I'll have a look at the body, if you don't mind."

"And we'll be glad to get rid of you when you finish," said the cop.

The other officers opened an aisle for him to pass through. They came to a closed door. The cop jerked his head toward it.

"He's in there," he said, "by himself."

"Thanks," said King. "I want to be alone with him."

He pushed open the door and stepped in. As he turned to close it, a sound coming from somewhere in that dimly lighted room literally froze him to the spot.

The door made a hollow noise as it shut but that wasn't what startled him. It was a low moan from behind.

He whirled round. The room was bare except for one piece of furniture. That was a marble slab on a pair of pedestals. And on that marble slab, sat a figure.

It was the figure of John Flint Waldorff.

A gasp escaped King's thin lips. He felt chills, like icy fingers, moving up his spine.

The big, broad-shouldered, gray-haired man wasn't merely sitting up on the slab. But he had swung his feet down to the floor. He was hunched over, his arms hanging limp, his shoulders bent and his head hanging as though his neck were broken.

It was actually two minutes but it seemed an eternity before King could make his feet track properly so that they would carry him to that gruesome figure.

Each step that he took was work. If he had done what his inward feelings prompted him to do, he would have turned and dashed out of that death room. But he forced himself on.

That low, moaning sound continued to come from the lips of John Flint Waldorff. As though the elderly man was trying to say something and couldn't.

Mumble—mumble—mumble!

Step by step King advanced upon him. But the form or body or living corpse or whatever was left of John Flint Waldorff seemed not to know even that another was in the room with him.

Then King was beside him. He reached out and touched the forehead.

He drew back instantly. The skin was cold as that of a corpse.

The body was naked, except for the sheet that had covered it, and which was now dragged partly from the slab and pulled across his middle.

KING STOOD there, staring for another minute. Listening to those mumbling sounds. Trying to make words out of them. Then he reached out and touched the left arm that hung limply on his side.

Again he drew back in astonishment. But this time not because that arm was icy cold. It was hot. As hot as the arm of a human running a temperature.

He stepped before the body and squatted on his one knee. But even in that position, he couldn't see directly into the slumped face.

"Mr. Waldorff!"

As King called his name, he touched his shoulder. It, too, was hot. He took hold, and shook.

"Mr. Waldorff!"

Still no answer. He shook the whole body heavily. Saw the muscles in the legs tighten. The legs moved to brace the body more firmly on the slab. But there was no other recognition that the man was at all alive.

King's hands trembled a little as he reached out for the head. The whole head was cold like the body of a corpse. But he held on this time. He raised the head. It came heavily as though it were almost severed from the body.

Now he could see the whole face. There were staring eyes. Eyes that seemed to see and at the same time, seemed to be looking through him. It made King's flesh crawl.

He could see the blackness of the throat, too. Black as a black eye.

He lowered the head and it flopped limp and hung there. King got to his feet. He felt shaky in every joint.

He moved to the left side of Waldorff and placed his hand on the naked chest. He could feel a very distinct beating of the heart. Evidently the man was alive and yet he was, at the same time, very dead.

King stood there and thought for a moment. He drew out a cigarette and lighted it. Took two puffs on it and stomped on it with his heel. It didn't taste natural. Nothing tasted natural inside that weird room.

If he could only get that body out so that the Doctor could make an examination of it. He glanced about the room for what seemed the hundredth time. There was no other door except the one by which he had entered. A small, heavily grated window was located high up on the outside wall.

But before he could plan how he might be able to get out through it, the door knob turned. A big cop stuck his head through the opening.

"Hey, it's time you was—" he broke off short.

"Holy Mother," he exploded.

He stood frozen there in the doorway for an instant. Other officers came rushing up behind him. Stared. Uttered gasps and exclamations. Then they poured into the room.

"What the devil goes on here?" the big cop demanded.

King shrugged.

"If you'll tell me," he said, "I'll be eternally grateful."

"Look here," shouted another cop. "You did this. You're under arrest for trying to—"

King nodded.

"Sure. Go ahead and tell me what I'm under arrest for," he said. "When I came in, Waldorff's body was sitting just like this. But I suppose you wouldn't believe that. So you think I brought him back to life. Go ahead and arrest me, if you want to give the old metropolis a good laugh. They'd get a kick out of a man being arrested for bringing someone back to life."

The big cop walked up gingerly beside the naked sitting body.

He touched his forehead as King had done. Drew back with a start.

"He's as cold as a corpse," he exclaimed.

Another officer touched Waldorff's left arm.

"He's burnin' up with fever," he declared.

Then the two cops looked at each other and King laughed hoarsely.

"Is he dead or alive?" he demanded.

The big cop dropped his hand to the left chest of Waldorff and stood there an instant.

"Holy Mother," he exclaimed. "His heart is pumpin'."

He began to nudge the body. Shook the shoulder nearest him roughly. There came only the action of the legs bracing the body as he moved it. And now that King was standing farther off at the side, he could see the muscles of the back tighten.

"Hey, Mr. Waldorff," said the big cop.

No movement of the head. No answer. Only that continuous low mumbling from the lips of the living corpse.

"Hey," the cop raised his voice and shook the body almost off the marble slab. "Hey, Mr. Waldorff."

"I wouldn't be too rough with him," King ventured.

"You mind your own business," snapped the cap. "I'm runnin' this show."

"Okay," said King, "but this might be some form of sleep that we don't know anything about. It's been suggested that either Black Magic or a Maya curse killed Mr. Waldorff. And here he is, partly returned to life after being pronounced dead. At least alive enough to swing his legs off the marble slab and sit up. If

you handle him too roughly, you might send him back perma-
nently into a relapse."

The cop glared, but stopped shaking the body. He whirled
to one of his men.

"Call the captain and get the surgeon here as quick as you
can," he ordered. "This is a case for a hospital, not a morgue."

A new plan came into King's nimble brain. He wasn't sure
if they were thinking of holding him but he must get out. He
turned to the big cop.

CHAPTER 8
THE VANISHING EIGHT

"CAN I ask a question?" he demanded.

"All right, newshound," snapped the cop. "What
is it?"

"Who saw this body first after it was brought to the morgue,
the family or the surgeon?"

"The family," snapped the cop. "The surgeon was busy. He
came in about a half hour after the family had left."

"Thanks," said King, "and where can I find the family now?"

"Can't you see I'm busy tryin' to think," snapped the big cop
in charge.

"Oh, that's what you call it when you make those faces," King
flung back. "Well, listen. Take a look at this."

He bent down and raised the head of John Flint Waldorff
gently. He pointed to the mark of the crescent and the circle put
there by the Doctor with an indelible pencil.

"I've got it on good authority that this mark is the mark of The Secret 6. It shows they're in on this job, too. I've made an agreement with the captain not to tell about that if he'll give me all the dope on the rest of the story. Now, do I get their address or don't I?"

The cop sulked for a moment.

"All right, "he barked. "They live in the big house up Fifth Avenue. The old mansion of the family. Now go to the devil, will yuh?"

"With pleasure," said King.

He turned toward the door. Felt the eyes of the other cops upon him. Were they going to hold him for what he might know or would they let him go without further suspicion?

He passed first one of the policemen and then another. They stared hard at him but that was all. Then he was out in the street and climbing hurriedly into his car.

The engine roared. He shot down the street and turned uptown. Next he swung over the bridge to Brooklyn and on out along the north main highway over Long Island.

The foot accelerator was down to the floor most of the time. Seventy, seventy-five. Eighty. And higher.

Minutes dragged by. His plan would work if everything came out right at the other end of the line.

It was growing late when he swerved into the secret drive through the wood that led near the cabin. He left the car in the bushes and leaped out.

The other members of The Secret 6 were sitting about the

one-room cabin. A fire burned briskly in the fireplace. Every face turned to stare at him.

Luga, curled up like a great dog in front of the fire, leaped to his feet.

"You all right, Master?" he pleaded.

"Okay, big boy," King smiled. "But I've got some news that will knock your hats off. Listen."

He told them briefly of his trip. Of his talk with the Maya Indian, Manaha. Of his close call with the reporter and his visit to the morgue.

"I'm afraid," he said, "things are getting pretty complicated now. When a man dies mysteriously, that's something. But when that man comes to life again, it's going almost too far for me."

The Bishop dropped his pipe as he sat up. The Doctor let his cigar fall from his mouth. The Key jumped as though he'd been shot. Shakespeare assumed the role of the scoffer.

"Come, come, now," Shakespeare said. "Surely you don't mean to say that you have actually witnessed the bringing back of the dead to life?"

KING NODDED.

"I don't mean anything else," he said. "Doctor, John Flint Waldorff was dead, wasn't he, when you examined him?"

The Doctor nodded.

"As dead as the medical profession can pronounce a man," he said with certainty.

"Then," said King, "a man has been brought back, at least partially, to life."

81

"What do you mean by partially?" demanded the Bishop. "Could it be that the second coming of miracles has arrived?"

"It sure looks like something of that kind," said King. "But I've got to get under motion. Shakespeare, I've got a job for you. Take this makeup off my face and make me look like myself."

"To be sure," said the old actor.

As Shakespeare worked on his face, removing the make-up, King explained:

"I got a pass from the captain of the substation to go to the morgue and inspect the body. I was a little curious about that sign of The Secret 6 that you put on Waldorff's forehead with an indelible pencil, Doctor."

"Had they tried to rub it off?" the Doctor asked.

"I think so, but they hadn't had much luck and apparently they must have thought it was something more than just an indelible pencil mark. It was still there very plainly."

The Bishop chuckled.

"I'd wager—if I was a wagering man—that the police are doing some sweating about that mark of ours. I wonder if they know that it is our secret sign?"

King nodded and grinned as Shakespeare finished cleaning his face of the make-up.

"If they don't, they're pretty dumb," King said. "I told them that I understood it was the sign of The Secret 6. And, also, I informed the officer stationed at the morgue that I was King of The Secret 6."

The Bishop's eyes twinkled and he chuckled deep down.

The Key exploded.

"Holy gee, you told 'em that? Boy, you sure got guts. And lots of luck. Some day you're goin' to put your neck in a hole that won't give."

"I know," laughed King, "but I couldn't resist that one." He recounted more fully what had happened in the morgue.

"And you mean there was nothing holding the corpse up there?" demanded the Doctor.

"Not a thing," said King, lighting a cigarette. "I thought he was in a half-sleep and I tried to shake him out of it. The only change I noticed was that his muscles tightened and his legs became more firmly planted on the floor so that I couldn't throw him off balance. But he never raised his head."

"Did you feel of his heart action?" asked the Doctor.

"Yes, and his heart was ticking very nicely, like any living human. But his head was as cold as a corpse."

"His head was cold?" exploded the Doctor. "You mean to say that his whole body was cold and still his heart was thumping regularly?"

"Not at all," said King. "That was the queerest part of it. His head was cold and his body from the neck down was hot, as if he had a high fever."

The Doctor sunk back in his chair.

"I give up," he said. "When Black and White Magic enter the picture, a medical man is out of the scene entirely."

"I'm not so sure," King said. "That's why I want you to come with me."

The Doctor leaned forward again with more interest.

"You know," he said, "it hadn't struck me so forcefully before.

But do you remember Waldorff's eyes were closed when we found him, as though he'd been asleep when he died?"

King and the rest nodded.

"It isn't natural to have the eyes closed in death," the Doctor said firmly. "I noticed that, but I had a strong feeling about Black Magic at the time. And that feeling is stronger now than it was then. You know—" he leaned forward still more on the edge of his chair—"what you say about his actions is much like the dead men laboring in the cane fields of Haiti at night. I'm afraid we're working on a hopeless job."

"I think," said King, "that this job has more of a human element than it seems to have."

"Yeah," said the Key. "Well, if you can show me anything human about the whole thing, I'll kiss your foot in the courthouse square on Palm Sunday."

"All right," said King. "Here are two things. First we get a warning from Flo about a couple of men plotting to get me. Key, do you know anything superhuman about a bird named Krano?"

The Key jerked upright.

"Krano," he snapped. "Holy he—"

"Ah, ah, ah," cut in the Bishop.

"I mean holy gee," the Key went on. "Krano is a guy that hires killin' done. Who was he talkin' to about you?"

"Flo couldn't find out his name. But she learned he was a killer leader who had men to do the work for him. Krano was telling him that they had to get me out of the way so the big boss could have clear sailing. Nothing superhuman about that, is there, Key?"

"Hel—I mean, goodness, no," stammered the Key.

"Then there's something else I found out," King hurried on. "You remember the money and securities that were in the unlocked safe on the yacht?"

Heads bobbed.

"When the police reached the yacht, the safe was empty. There wasn't anybody on the boat from the time we left it until the police arrived."

"What a crazy guy you were for not takin' that dough instead of leavin' it for the police," the Key sputtered.

"I'm sure the police didn't take it," King said. "Some of them might stoop to bribes, but I doubt if any would stoop so low as to steal the contents of a safe with a dead man in the room."

King grinned as he glanced from the Key to the Doctor.

"Do either one of these things I've just told you sound like Black Magic or a Maya curse?" he asked.

"Sounds to me like the Maya Indian has got some thugs to help him and is guilty as he—as the dickens," said the Key.

"Manaha is telling the truth," said King. "I'm satisfied with that. And now, Doctor, if you'll take a little ride with me, we'll talk to some of the Waldorff family and maybe you can get another look at John Flint Waldorff in the flesh. They were planning to take him to a hospital the last I heard."

The Doctor leaped to his feet and tossed his cigar butt into the fireplace.

"IT SOUNDS more interesting now," he admitted. "Just a minute until I get a handful of cigars and I'll be with you."

He stuffed them into his pocket and turned toward the door.

"We're not going to fly, are we?" he demanded suddenly.

King laughed. "Not this time, Doctor," he said. "I think we'll take your sedan this time."

"Wait," explained Shakespeare, "don't you want another make-up?"

King shook his head.

"Thanks, no," he said. "This time I'm going just as King."

Then, before anyone could raise too much objection or stop him, King and the Doctor were gone into the night with Luga watching them wistfully from the door.

As they walked rapidly through the darkened woods toward the place where the cars stood, the Doctor asked, "Just what do you think I can do?"

King shrugged. "I'm not sure that I know," he said. "But we've got to cover every possibility. You're a doctor and you've also seen voodoo Black Magic work. You know considerably more than the police surgeon does because he thinks that John Flint Waldorff was killed like his brother two months ago, by choking."

King felt the Doctors eyes upon him.

"You're beginning to believe in Black Magic yourself," he charged.

King shrugged. "If it wasn't for those two things, the men trying to get me out of the way and the disappearance of the money from the safe on the *Pagan*, I'm afraid I'd have a lot more respect for Black Magic."

They walked on in silence, reached the sedan. The Doctor

drove. They turned out of the long, bedrock drive and onto the main highway, first making sure that no cars were in sight.

The Doctor made that fast little sedan do plenty of miles. It was nearing midnight when they crossed the bridge into the Bronx and started downtown.

"Where do we go first?" he asked.

"I think we'll take in the home of the Waldorffs on Fifth Avenue," King said. "Know where it is?"

The Doctor nodded and swung 'round a corner to head through Central Park. While King had talked at the cabin, he had changed into another suit, discarding the one with the burned coat.

A clock was striking the hour of twelve as they stopped in front of the Waldorff Mansion. It was one of those very old Fifth Avenue mansions that cover a whole city block. A great wall of stone topped by an iron spike fence surrounded the property.

The Doctor stopped the car in front and they stepped to the sidewalk.

"Got any idea what you're going to run into?" he asked.

King shook his head.

"Not the slightest. Perhaps you'd better go first and introduce yourself as a doctor of science interested in the case from a scientific angle. If the place isn't full of police, I'll follow. Ask if you may see Miss Constance Waldorff."

The Doctor nodded and, advancing up the great stone steps, rang the bell. King stood behind him in the shadow.

Presently the door opened and a butler with a white, scared face blinked out at him.

"I would like to see Miss Constance Waldorff," the Doctor boomed.

The butler moved as though to close the door.

"I'm sorry, sir," he said, "but Miss Waldorff is not seeing any newspaper men."

"I'm not a newspaper man," the Doctor boomed louder still. He slipped his foot in the crack of the door, kept it from being closed. "I'm a doctor of science. I'd like to see Miss Waldorff to inquire if I may help."

The butler was persistent.

"I'm sorry, sir, but Miss Constance is not—"

A female voice cut him off. And at almost the same instant a young woman put in an appearance. The butler moved aside and opened the door with a bow.

"A doctor of science?" inquired the girl. "I'll see him."

She stood there for a split second with the light from the hall falling upon her slim figure. She was very good looking. The big cop at the morgue hadn't overrated her in the least, King decided. The Doctor bowed. King followed him in.

The girl looked at King, hesitated for an instant. But he was already inside and helping the butler close the door.

The Doctor spoke with another bow.

"I am simply known as the Doctor," he said. "And this is my assistant—er—"

The girl frowned at the hesitation. King smiled and stepped forward.

"Miss Waldorff," he said. "We're here to help if we can. If we can be alone for a few minutes, I believe I can explain everything to your satisfaction."

Connie Waldorff's eyes were not wet or red with weeping for her mysteriously dead uncle, as one might expect. She seemed a bit nervous but otherwise in very good control of her feelings.

She shot keen glances at both men from flashing brown eyes, then she nodded.

"If you gentlemen are newspaper men, I can assure you now that you're wasting your time."

"I can assure you," said King, "that neither the Doctor nor myself are interested in newspapers in any way. We are telling the absolute truth when we say we wish to help. May we have five minutes—" he glanced at the butler— "in private?"

King smiled again. For another moment the girl hesitated. It was hard to resist that grin when King let it go gay. She answered with a smile of her own. A worn, tired smile but a smile nevertheless.

"Five minutes, then," she said. "And you give me your word of honor, that you will go at the end of five minutes if I wish it?"

Both King and the Doctor agreed.

"Very well," said Connie Waldorff. "Let's go into the library. This way. We can be alone there."

SHE LED the way through a partly open door into a heavy paneled room that was lined with books on two sides. On the third side were a row of oil paintings. She waited until they had entered, then closed the door.

"Won't you sit down," she asked, seating herself in an overstuffed leather chair. "We may as well all be comfortable for the five minutes."

"You must feel very sure of yourself," King began, "to trust yourself with two men, alone, who you have never seen before."

"My judgment of men has not often been wrong," she explained. "But you're wasting time. What was it you came to see me about, please?"

King studied her for some time. Then he smiled again.

"I believe, Miss Waldorff," he began, "that we can trust you with a secret which is very important to both the Doctor and myself. Am I right?"

"If you can prove to me that you are here to help me and Cousin Henry and George, you may rest assured that your secret will not leave this house," Miss Waldorff said.

King bowed. "Miss Waldorff, you have heard, perhaps, of The Secret 6?"

The girl's eyes widened ever so slightly.

"Of course. But who are they? That seems to be the question." Then she leaned forward a little and King felt her brown eyes boring into his face. "You know, I believe I've seen you before somewhere."

"Or perhaps my picture," King corrected. "You may recall the Red Shadow case?"

"Yes, of course," gasped the girl. "You—you couldn't be—"

"King," said the leader of the band. "And this is the Doctor. One of our band of six. You see, as we told you, we are not newspaper men."

The girl's right fist doubled over a small lace handkerchief.

That was the only change of emotion that she showed until she said, "I—I'm so glad. I've been wishing I could reach you and your band ever since we first heard about you. My father died very mysteriously two months ago. And now my Uncle John has passed away and the most terrible thing has happened. Cousin Henry received a telephone call from the—the morgue, saying Uncle John had returned to life and they were taking him to the hospital. They said he was like a living dead man."

"Yes," said King. "I was the first to find him in that condition!"

He recounted what had happened so far, then he asked, "Who is your Cousin Henry and George that you mentioned?"

"Cousin Henry was my father's cousin. George is his son," said the girl. "They have gone to the hospital where they've taken Uncle John. I'm expecting to hear from them any minute now."

Suddenly her eyes took on a frightened look. Up to then she had been a composed woman under perfect self-control. Now she changed suddenly to a frightened little girl seeking protection.

"Please," she begged, "tell me what you think. Do you think this is a Maya curse brought upon us because our ancestors took gold from the ancient Mayan temples?"

King didn't hesitate for a split second. He shook his head.

"No, there is too much modern human element entering into the affair. Even before we started investigating this crime, there were men hired to kill me.

He saw her eyes widen. There was no need of going further into detail. He asked her a question in return.

"Perhaps while we are waiting to hear from your Cousin

Henry," he said, "we might go into your family history. Would you mind beginning with the first Waldorff who went to Yucatan to explore the Mayan temples?"

"I'll gladly do anything that will help," the girl said.

She turned and pointed to an old oil painting of a man with a beard.

"That," she said, "is my great-grandfather, Ezra Waldorff. He went down to Yucatan a little before the Civil War and was quite successful logging mahogany. It was during his lumber work that he ran across some interesting ruined temples.

"He sent north for his two sons—John Waldorff, who was my grandfather and Ezra Waldorff, Junior, who was my great-uncle.

"This was the year before the Civil War. My great-uncle Ezra was in the slave-trading business. Great-grandfather never liked it and he was very disappointed when Uncle Ezra wrote back to him and said if he'd give him his share of what inheritance he might get, he would go his own way, or something of that kind."

King nodded. "I assume that your great-grandfather and your great-uncle Ezra didn't get along so well together," he said.

The girl agreed. "I believe that great-grandfather had had several arguments about the methods he used in slave-trading," she said. "At any rate, great-grandfather paid him off and my grandfather, John Waldorff—his picture is over there—went down to help."

King glanced at the picture she designated. It was a painting of a man with dark hair and a lined, weathered face. He wore a heavy mustache, and there was something about the face that reminded him of John Flint Waldorff.

The girl went on.

"Great-grandfather Waldorff died shortly after he and my grandfather discovered the rich deposit of gold that is the basis for the family money. He died of black fever, but there was talk about a curse."

"How many children did your grandfather have?" King asked.

"Two," said the girl. "My uncle, John Flint Waldorff, and my father, who died two months ago."

"Where does Cousin Henry enter into the picture?"

Cousin Henry is great-uncle Ezra's son. Some time after great-grandfathers death, his two sons got closer together. Uncle Ezra made a fortune in the slavery business before the Civil War stopped him."

"And Cousin Henry was his only heir?"

"Yes."

"So that left Cousin Henry and his son pretty well fixed?"

"I believe so," said the girl. "I know Cousin Henry made a trip to Yucatan not long ago. He found some gold there, I think, although the Waldorffs don't discuss money matters very much."

A bell jangled softly.

"Excuse me," Miss Waldorff said, "the 'phone."

King spied the instrument standing on the library table. He leaped to hand it to her. She took it with a note of thanks and lifted the instrument from the standard, uttered a soft "hello."

Then she was listening. King watched her face, it was growing whiter by the second.

"Why—why," she gasped, "that's terrible. I can't understand."

She hung up the receiver and her lips formed a firm, hard line across her teeth.

"Cousin Henry called," she explained. "He—he says the ambulance left the morgue with Uncle John. When it reached the hospital, Uncle John was gone."

CHAPTER 9
A DEAD MAN TALKS

FOR SEVERAL seconds the room seemed to be electrified. King shot a glance at the Doctor. But the Doctor, in turn, was staring at King. He shook his head slowly, as though in wonder.

"Do you mean to say, Miss Waldorff," he demanded, "that John Flint Waldorff's body vanished from the ambulance somewhere between the morgue and the hospital? Wasn't there an attendant riding with him?"

The girl shook her head. She was sitting up straight, her hands pressed together in her lap. Her brown eyes wore a baffled expression.

"I don't know about the attendant," she said. "Cousin Henry told me that Uncle John had disappeared somewhere between the—the morgue and the hospital. He is returning here just as soon as he can."

King licked his lips, then he got out a pack of cigarettes, rose and offered them to Miss Waldorff.

Her hand trembled as she took one. King's own hand wasn't

any too steady as he held a match for her. Not a word was spoken until she lighted hers, then she said, "Thank you."

He took one and lighted it. The Doctor bit off the end of a cigar sagely and lighted it. King strode to the end of the library and back to his chair, but he didn't sit down. He walked to the mantle of the fireplace and leaned one arm against it, staring into the blackened interior of the grate.

Constance Waldorff joined him.

"Can't you do something?" she asked.

"I'd be delighted to do something," said King, "if I could think of anything to do. I'm afraid we'll simply have to wait until your Cousin Henry returns. Did he say where he was phoning from?"

"No," said the girl.

They stood in silence, one on either end of the great fireplace mantle.

"King," said the Doctor at length, "you saw John Flint Waldorff sitting on the marble slab. Would you say that he had the power to walk?"

King nodded.

"He certainly had strength enough to keep himself from toppling over when that big cop shook him," he said. "And the cop didn't shake him very gently either. Yes, I'd say he had the strength to walk."

"Then why couldn't he have escaped from the back of the ambulance himself? Why couldn't he be roaming about the streets of New York somewhere between the morgue and the hospital?"

"He could," King admitted, "if your guess is right. That is, if

95

there was no attendant to stop him. Suppose I call the police sub-station and find out if—"

He stopped short as a soft sound came from the hall. Constance Waldorff jumped as though she were shot.

"There's someone at the door now," she said. "Perhaps it's Cousin Henry."

The girl ran across the library, flung the door wide. A large form stood on the threshold. He was a distinguished looking gentleman somewhat past middle age. His hair was gray at the temples. His features were regular and pleasant.

"Oh, Cousin Henry," the girl exclaimed. "I'm so glad you've come."

She flew into his arms.

"There, there," the man said, patting her shoulder. "We've done everything we can for the present."

Miss Waldorff moved a little away from him then.

"Where's George?" she asked. "Didn't he come back with you?"

"George," repeated the man. "You must have forgotten. George went out earlier this evening."

"Oh, yes. I remember now."

Henry was staring past her at King and the Doctor.

"You have company, my dear," he said. "These are not—"

"I'm so sorry," said Miss Waldorff, getting hold of herself. "I almost forgot. These are two gentlemen who have come to help us. But you must promise to keep their identity a secret." She closed the door. "This is King of The Secret 6 and this is the Doctor of the same band."

Henry Waldorff hesitated a moment, glanced from one to the other. Then he walked forward and extended his hand to each cordially.

"I remember your face, King, in the papers," he said. "Mighty nice of you to come. What have you learned so far?"

King smiled rather sheepishly.

"So far, Mr. Waldorff," he said, "we haven't learned much but a jumble of information that doesn't fit any too well into one puzzle."

"I see," said Henry Waldorff. "Well, sit down. Perhaps if we all try to look at this thing calmly, we may be able to help each other. Is there anything I can tell you?"

"One thing I'd like very much to know," boomed the Doctor. "Was there an attendant in the ambulance that took John Flint Waldorff to the hospital?"

Henry shook his head.

"The police told me that no one would ride inside with him. If there had been an attendant, we might be able to throw more light on his disappearance."

King's eyes narrowed.

"Mr. Waldorff," he said, "I was at the morgue and saw John Flint Waldorff sitting on the edge of the slab. That was quite some time ago. How does it happen that his disappearance has just come to light?"

Henry Waldorff shot a quick glance at him. Then he smiled.

"You'll have to excuse me for appearing angry at first, Mr.—er—King," he explained. "But from your tone of voice, it sounded as though you were putting me on the witness stand. Of course, I realize your eagerness to solve the crime."

"You know how the police like to finish their job. And you can readily understand that they would catch the very devil if they admitted that the occupant of an ambulance had slipped out of the back door because no policeman had nerve enough to stay inside with him."

"That is what happened. There were two officers on the driver's seat of the police ambulance that took John away from the morgue. When they reached the hospital and found that their ambulance was empty, they turned around and retraced their movements, hoping to find him wandering about the streets."

"They spent considerable time hunting for him. Finally they had to report to headquarters and I only received the information a short time ago."

King nodded reluctantly.

"That seems to take care of that point completely," he admitted.

"And at the same time," cut in the Doctors booming voice, "it ties things up into a tighter knot than they were in before."

"Exactly, gentlemen," agreed Henry Waldorff. "I must confess I'm at the end of my rope. I can't think of—"

The jangling of the telephone cut in on his conversation. Henry picked it up.

"Yes, this is the Waldorff residence… Henry Waldorff speaking… What's that… gone! Good heavens. For hours, perhaps yes, of course… I'm really not surprised to hear it, but the method…. Thank you, indeed."

He hung up the receiver and turned with an air of finality, as though something were settled in his own mind.

"I believe," he said, "that we are coming very close to a solution. That was the captain of the police sub-station where Manaha was held. He escaped a little while after a newspaper man called on him."

KING STARED. "Escaped! How could he get out of that jail?"

"The captain tells me there was a grated window high in his cell that opened on an alley back of the jail; it was taken out as clean as though a bolt of lightning had struck it."

Henry Waldorff sat down, shook his head.

"I would have sworn you could trust Manaha with anything," he said.

He stopped and stared at the floor, thinking hard. Suddenly he tensed as if he were listening. King had opened his mouth to defend the Indian, then he, too, listened.

From somewhere in that house, apparently from beneath the thickly carpeted floor of the library, came a heavy footstep.

Thud!

There was a short, still interval. Then again it came.

Thud!

There could be no mistake now. Someone was walking up the cellar stairs. Someone with legs that moved slowly like a great automaton and with shoes that sounded heavy as lead.

Thud!

Another sound interrupted the pacing of those weird heavy

feet. The front door burst open and the voice of a young man called from the hall.

"Dad, oh, Dad!"

Henry Waldorff leaped to his feet and stepped lightly to the library door. Opening it, he motioned a young man inside, shut the door with a trace of irritation.

"My son, George," he whispered. "George, be quiet. Take a chair. Something is happening. Listen."

George was past twenty-one. Except for a rather weak chin, he wasn't a bad looking chap and resembled his father quite strongly. He smiled at Constance, then as that *thud* came again, he tensed.

"What's that?" he demanded.

"Shhh. Someone coming up the cellar stairs."

The face of George Waldorff went a little white. He grew rigid. Everyone was listening again.

King sat motionless. His eyes shifted from father to son and back again. Neither was moving. Henry Waldorff was staring down at the floor of the library as though looking at the direction from which the sound came would help him to hear it more plainly.

Thud! Thud! Thud!

Even through the closed door of the library, they could hear the knob of another door, out in the hall, rattle. One more *thud* and they heard the door opening.

From the hall there came a piercing yell. King and the Doctor leaped to their feet and flung open the library door.

As they burst out into the hall, with the others close behind, they saw the butler flattened against the wall in horror, his face deathly white. His hands were outstretched as though to keep something away. They turned and followed his gaze.

John Flint Waldorff was walking toward them very heavy, like a man in a trance. His head was bowed on his chest. His shoulders dropped forward a little and his arms hung limp. It made King think of the way a great ape might walk if he had a broken neck and could still move.

Thud!

Another step and then another. Great strides with a ghastly automatic swing that was brutally inhuman.

He was heading straight for the library door. King and the Doctor stood there, blocking his way. But he came on with that steady, determined tread as though he would walk through them rather than be stopped. They backed away before him. Backed into the library.

Thud! Thud!

John Flint Waldorff came on, entered the library. He made an effort to raise his head. When that failed, he tried to talk. Mumbled sounds issued from his lips.

Mumble—mumble—mumble!

Then gradually, out of the jumble of sound, came audible words. Words that struck with an air of new horror.

"Jim—Jim—needs—help!"

For the moment, it seemed no one could speak except the girl. She stepped before the walking corpse that was her uncle.

"Father is dead," she said. "He can't be—"

Then she suddenly cringed and darted back. For John Flint

101

Waldorff had lifted his right arm. It wasn't limp now. It was rigid and trembling, and it pointed straight at her.

"Jim—your father—needs you."

The girl was shaking violently. King stepped over and put his arm about her in case she should faint. But she didn't. Instead, she answered her uncle.

"But father has been buried for two months, Uncle John."

"I—know," said the corpse. "Jim needs you. Maya curse. Curse killed me. Look—at me. Jim needs you. Go—to vault. Jim can't get out—to—tell—who dies—next."

CHAPTER 10
DEATH LEAVES A TOMB

THEN JOHN Flint Waldorff did the most human thing he had done since his death. He turned and, with his head still bent, looked about for a chair. He found a comfortable one near the fireplace. His legs moved. He walked to it heavy and sat down, slumping in almost the same position in which he had been found on board his yacht. He closed his eyes.

The Doctor stepped over to him instantly. John Flint Waldorff didn't move when the physician placed a hand on his chest over his heart.

"He's alive, all right," the Doctor murmured. "At least, his heart is pumping."

King turned hastily to Henry Waldorff.

"Where is the vault that John Flint Waldorff just mentioned?" he demanded.

The girl cut in before the older man could answer.

"It's in Woodlawn cemetery. My grandfather built it and everyone in the family who dies is laid there. Please, let's hurry. Uncle John must know something that he can't explain. My father is—"

King nodded.

"The Doctor and I will go just as soon as we can find out how to get in," he assured her. "I doubt that the gates are open. We had better 'phone the caretaker. You do that, Doctor, will you? Be discreet so he won't get suspicious and call the police. The mention of the Waldorff name ought to quiet him." The Doctor nodded and went to the 'phone. King went on curtly. "Do you know where the vault key is?"

"Yes," said the girl. "It is kept in this desk. It hasn't been out since father was buried there. Cousin Henry, you know where the key is. Get it, won't you, please, and hurry."

"Of course, my dear," Henry Waldorff said. He opened the desk and searched about. "Let me see, I've forgotten which drawer it is kept in." He began pulling out one drawer and then another. "Oh, yes. I have it. This is it, isn't it, Connie?"

The girl nodded at sight of the large key which he held up, then she turned to King.

"I'm going with you, of course," she informed him. There was no chance for argument, but King brought one forward.

"I'm not so sure that it would be for the best. Wouldn't it be better if the Doctor and I went first and then—"

"I'm going," the girl flung back as she went out into the hall and picked up a wrap from a chair.

103

"I suggest," said Henry Waldorff, "that we all go together. That is, if you wish to go, George."

The face of the young man was ashen white.

"You bet I'll go," George said instantly. "I wouldn't stay here alone for all the money in the world."

The Doctor was still at the telephone. They waited silently until he had finished. "It's O.K.," he said. "Very irregular, but the Waldorff name sort of awed him."

King jerked his head toward the quiet form of John Flint.

"What do you think should be done about him?" he asked.

The Doctor turned to Henry Waldorff.

"Can you lock the library door from the outside?"

Henry nodded.

"Then I think that's the proper thing to do," he concluded. "I don't see what a hospital can do for John Flint Waldorff. And he seems to be resting easily where he is."

They filed out of the library one after another. Henry Waldorff came last, carrying the key to the cemetery vault. He closed the library door behind him and locked it.

"We have a small sedan right at the door that will hold all five of us easily," King ventured.

The others nodded and hurried out into the street.

King slipped behind the wheel and started the motor. The Doctor sat next to him. The other three took the back seat. The car moved off.

"Know where Woodlawn cemetery is?" King asked the Doctor.

The big man nodded. "I'll point out the turns," he said. And did.

As they drove, both stared ahead in silence. Once King heard a sobbing sound from the back seat. That was Constance. Little wonder she was breaking down after an ordeal like this.

He pressed the accelerator to the floor when he had the chance. But he must be careful not to be picked up for speeding. Many police officers would recognize him now with no disguising makeup on his face.

Part way there he turned to the Doctor and spoke softly. So softly that those in the rear seat could not hear.

"Did you notice anything queer tonight?"

The Doctor turned as though he'd been shot.

"Queer," he hissed back. "I haven't seen anything in the last twelve hours that wasn't queer."

"I mean about the thudding sound of John Flint's footsteps."

The Doctor stopped to think.

"Did you notice," King went on, "that the footsteps stopped when young Waldorff came in the front door?"

"By George," exclaimed the Doctor softly, "I remember now. They did. I didn't hear them again until George was in the library and the door was closed."

"Might be well to keep an eye on young George. I don't know why," said King, "and I'm probably crazy."

"I think you are but maybe we'll all be crazy before this is over," hissed the Doctor. "Looks to me as though the old boy was playing 'possum."

"You mean Henry?" demanded King.

The living dead man stood clutching the bars of the tomb.

"Lord, no," said the Doctor. "I mean John Flint himself."

King thought that one over; then shook his head.

"That still doesn't make sense. He'd have a tough time stopping his heart from beating and then starting it up again—at will."

"Nothing makes sense," growled the Doctor. "Here's the gate where we turn into the cemetery.

KING SPUN the wheel and they crunched tires on the gravel drives. A flashlight shone on them for an instant, then the great iron gates were pulled open. As they drove in, King got a glimpse of an old, curious-eyed man standing behind them. The caretaker, evidently. He waved them on.

Henry Waldorff spoke from the rear.

"I'll direct you," he said. "It's a little way back from here. Now turn left next. That's correct."

King followed directions.

"We're getting close," Constance said in a voice that was none too steady. "Suppose you drive straight for the vault when I point it out to you. Then our headlights will shine on the doors."

"Good idea," agreed King. He drove on a little farther. Then he heard the girl's voice.

"Oh, what's that? Turn here. To the right. Quick."

King spun the wheel to the right. His headlights rimmed the edge of a great granite vault, swung farther and farther toward the iron gate that he could see dimly.

There was something behind those iron gates. A figure of a man—or was it an ape?

Bam!

The lights swung full on the gates and that figure behind them.

King heard a muffled cry from the back seat. Before he could slap on the brakes to bring the car to a full stop, the rear door was opening and Constance Waldorff was leaping out. She struck something rough in the road and fell.

King jumped out, but before he could reach her, she was on her feet again and running headlong for that weird figure.

"Father," she called. "Father."

Everyone was out of the car now and running toward the tomb. The girl reached it first. King saw her in the light of the headlights. He was right behind her as she put out her hands and touched the face of the ghastly figure.

With a moan, she sprang back. The others stopped and stared at the unearthly spectacle.

It seemed as if the girl had recognized at least the form of her father. Her father, who had been dead and buried in the vault at least two months ago.

The living dead man stood clutching the bars. He seemed not to see any of the group before him. His legs were spread wide apart for support. The hands that clutched the iron bars were bony. His head was bowed, chin on his chest, just as John Flint Waldorff's head had been.

But King could see the upper part of the face quite clearly.

It was a horrible picture. Two glowing eyes reflected the light of the headlamps. The rest of the face was covered with green mold so that the nose and mouth blended together in a mask of horror.

There were two patches where the mold had come off. That was where Constance Waldorff had taken her father's face in her hands. The lips, surrounded by mold, were parted and were moving. King whirled to the others, caught Henry Waldorff by the arm.

"Quick," he said. "Let's have the key to the vault."

Henry Waldorff hesitated.

"Do you think it would be safe to—to let him out?"

"He's coming out," King snapped. "The man's alive, or partly so. A tomb is no place to lock up a living man."

Henry Waldorff advanced with apparent unwillingness. He placed the key in the lock and turned. King pulled the iron door open and stepped in beside the standing form of James Waldorff. The tomb was filled with a dank, musty smell. But there was no odor of rotting flesh.

He took hold of the arm of the living dead man. The clothing felt strange, damp and musty; but the arm inside was hot. He could feel that through the coat sleeve.

He stood there for a moment, staring at the mold-covered face. A thought flashed through his brain. Without speaking out loud, he said to himself, "Perhaps I'd better wipe off the mold."

To his amazement, the mumbling sound from those ghastly lips formed slurred words.

"Please—wipe off—mold."

King tensed, withdrew his hand before he know what he was doing. That was the queerest thing that had happened yet. Perhaps it was only coincidence. But James Waldorff had read the very thoughts in his mind.

King took out his handkerchief and began wiping the mold from the face and neck. He had to lift the head in order to make a good clean job of it. The face was as cold as that of John Flint had been. The body was hot in the same way. And as the head was raised, King saw that the throat was black.

With the mold all wiped off, he once more took hold of James Waldorff's arm.

"We're going to take you home, Mr. Waldorff," he said.

"Yes, home," mumbled James Waldorff. He stopped stock still for an instant. Then as though the thought had just come to him, he said, "I—have—things—to tell."

King urged him on out of the tomb.

"That will be fine," he declared. "When we get you home, we'll be glad to listen."

When they stepped from the tomb, Constance Waldorff came forward and took her fathers other arm. Together she and King escorted him, very slowly, to the car.

King was just about to suggest that Waldorff sit in the front seat between himself and the Doctor, when the walking corpse spoke again.

"Sit in front seat. My body—is—hot. It—would not be—well to frighten—Constance—unduly."

King stared at him.

"That's funny. I was just about to suggest the same thing for the same reason."

NOT A word was spoken on the way back to the Waldorff Mansion. James Waldorff sat rigidly between King and the

Doctor, his head lolling limply on his chest. From behind came the gentle sobbing of Connie.

As they helped the living dead man into his house, the butler peered from the back of the hall. He ducked from sight with a terrified cry as he saw his former master entering. Silently, Henry Waldorff unlocked the library door. John Flint was still slumped in the great chair by the fireplace, apparently asleep.

"I think it would be well if I had some coffee prepared," Henry said gravely. He went out for a few moments.

"Coffee will be served shortly," he said when he came back. "Now, perhaps we can get on with this—this story that you have, Jim?"

The head of old James Waldorff bobbed on his chest. They had placed him in a chair facing John Flint, but he hardly seemed to notice. In fact, he seemed in a daze until Henry spoke. Then he raised his eyes.

The first gray rays of dawn were just filtering through the unshuttered windows.

"You—will all—sit down," he began. "I have important information—for you—all who will—listen."

Up to then the only ones who had been sitting were James and his sleeping brother, John. Now the rest obeyed.

King glanced around at the group. It was cool, but in spite of that fact, he noticed Henry Waldorff mopping his brow with a handkerchief.

Then very slowly, with his head still bowed, James Waldorff struggled to his feet and stood there blinking at them from under his lids.

"You are aware," he began, "that the Maya curse was put on us. It has—killed me—and my brother, John. We have come back to life to tell—what our departed souls—have learned."

The room was still as death. The breathing of the talking corpse and the low snoring sound from John Flint sounded like screaming buzz saws.

Henry mopped his brow and leaned heavily against the back of his chair.

"There is but one way," James Waldorff droned on, "to stop this curse. The Waldorff fortune was started with some ten million dollars in gold stolen from the Temple of Azrah, the ancient Maya temple of bats. It is forty miles southwest of the present city of Izamal."

"You must return this money. Take ten million dollars in gold or currency or securities to the Temple of Azrah and leave it between the pillars to the right of the entrance. Then the curse of the Maya will be lifted."

The living dead man took a heavy breath and went on.

"The sooner the ten million dollars is returned, the sooner the curse of the Maya will be lifted. There is a lake close to the temple where an airplane might land. I would advise that you go by plane."

King leaped to his feet.

"I'll go," he said. "I've got a fast plane and I can take off in an hour or so."

The lolling head on James Waldorff's chest moved sidewise.

"No, that would not do. It must be one of the Waldorff family who takes down the gold."

"Very well," agreed King. "I'll go down to look into this business, anyway. I don't like the sound of it. I'm leaving for Yucatan as soon as I can get to my plane."

The arm of James Waldorff came up suddenly, stiffly.

"Wait," he cried. "I have more to tell. If you do that, the curse of the Maya will be upon you and your Secret 6 band."

"How do you know anything about me and The Secret 6?" King demanded.

James Waldorff swayed, paused, then he said, "My soul, in its wanderings, has learned much. I tell you if you go there, you will be cursed by Maya evil. And more than that. The Maya curse is marking this household again."

He tried to raise his eyes and glance about the room, but it was too much of an effort. However, his words left everyone frozen where they sat or stood. Then suddenly King was staring at Henry Waldorff. Staring at his throat; it was growing dark.

At the same instant, James Waldorff pointed a finger at him, and his mumbling voice carried the sting of death.

"You, Henry," he said, "are the next to fall under the Maya curse. Very soon you will die. Look at your throat. It is growing dark already. Before long—"

James Waldorff suddenly stopped speaking. He began to mumble as though he had lost his power of speech. He sat down limply in a chair and slowly fell into a deep slumber like his brother, John.

All eyes turned to Henry. He had lolled back in his chair. His eyes were closed. His head was tipped back and his throat was growing darker in color.

113

The Doctor hurried over, placed his big hand on the afflicted man's chest. After a moment, he looked up.

"Henry Waldorff," he said slowly, "is dead."

CHAPTER 11
GHOST MISSION

"DEAD!" THE sound of that voice echoed through the library like shouts of invading soldiers in a cathedral. It was the voice of George Waldorff, son of the man whom the Doctor had just pronounced dead. He rushed to his father.

"No, no," he called out. "You can't be, Dad. No. I—"

King grasped the young man's arm firmly and pulled him away.

"I'm afraid," he said calmly, "that you'll have to face the facts."

George stared at him for a second. Then he fell into the nearest chair and began sobbing.

King turned to Constance Waldorff. The girl's eyes were a little red and showed signs of fear, but there was an admirable calm about her.

"I wonder if we can do anything more here?" King said.

The girl hesitated.

"I mean," King said, "perhaps we can think more clearly in some other room. Your father and your uncle seem to be resting quietly. Your cousin Henry has been pronounced dead. There is apparently nothing more we can do for him. Shall we go out into some other part of the house?"

The girl nodded. "Please."

King took George by the arm and helped him to his feet.

"Come on, old man," he said. "I know it's tough, but there's nothing we can do here."

The girl led the way out into the hall and down it to a smaller room that was obviously a den. There, when George was deposited in a chair, she faced King.

"Please," she begged, "haven't you any idea what we can do about this?"

King hesitated. "Miss Waldorff," he said at last, "just how firmly do you believe your father's statement that the curse will be broken when the money is returned?"

Her eyes widened.

"Why, my father said it. He uttered the words. I've never known him to tell a lie in my life."

"Could you raise ten million dollars within the next few hours?"

She bit her lip.

"I—I don't know," she admitted. "You see, my father's estate is still tied up in the courts. He has only been—dead—for two months. I had quite a bit of money left me by my grandfather. I don't know how much that amounts to—now. I'll have to see my attorney."

"Do you think," King asked, "that you should take your father's advice and bring that money down to the Azrah temple?"

"Why—why, yes," the girl said. "I suppose so. Everything has happened so swiftly I hardly know what to say. My head aches so I can't think and when I do, everything is so mixed up."

King nodded. "I know exactly how you feel. But I was think-

115

ing this. If you wish me to, I'll fly the money down to Yucatan. You can go with me if you like, although it might be advisable to stay here. Our hideout is on the north shore of Long Island. My plane is there. I'll go out and get the plane and meet you at Floyd Bennett Field in two hours. Will that do?"

The girl hesitated.

"I'm afraid I couldn't have much information by then," she said. "Suppose we make it three hours."

"Good," agreed King. "We'll go back and get the plane ready. There's nothing more that we can do here at present?"

The girl shook her head.

"I suppose I'd better call the police—about Cousin Henry?"

King nodded.

"I imagine they'll have to come into the case again before long," he said. "Yes, I think I'd call them if I were you, when you got around to it. I don't see that there is any hurry, however." He turned to the Doctor. "Shall we go? And don't worry, Miss Waldorff, I'm sure everything is going to work out all right."

"Thank you," she said, and walked with them to the front door.

When they had climbed into the sedan and were moving off, the Doctor shook his head.

"You certainly are an optimist, King. Telling that girl that you were sure everything was coming out all right. I've never seen so many things go the way you least expected them to in all my life."

King took a long breath and turned across the bridge.

"After all," he said, "I couldn't tell her that I thought everything was hopeless and just to lay down and die, could I?"

"No," agreed the Doctor, "I don't suppose you could. Just what do you make of the whole deal?"

King grinned.

"Now I'll ask one. Did you ever hear of a soul leaving his body, fluttering around until it had picked up some very nice pieces of gossip and then returning to the body and relaying the gossip to the public?"

"Don't be silly," growled the Doctor.

"All right," said King. "Then tell me how James Waldorff found out that you and I were from The Secret 6. He was between us every minute of the time since we took him from the vault. Then without warning, he stands up there and—"

"Yes, yes," snapped the Doctor. "I was there and heard it all."

A long silence as they hit Long Island and rolled on in the clear morning air on the main north shore highway.

"Just what do you figure you're going to profit by flying down to Yucatan?" he asked at length.

"For one thing," King said, "I'm following directions given by James Waldorff."

"Bunk," said the Doctor. "Pure bunk!"

"So what?" asked King. "You wouldn't by any means be hinting that James Waldorff was putting on this whole show to get his own money, would you?"

The Doctor turned in the front seat and glared at him.

"You wouldn't," he retorted, "by any chance be hinting that this is the work of a human being, would you? If you are and can prove it, all the historians and scientists and theologians have got a powerful lot to learn about resurrections."

The plane vaulted over King's car and began to bank.

Another long pause. Then King asked, "Do you think Connie Waldorff can raise the money?"

"So it's Connie now," the Doctor smiled. "Well, so far as her raising the money, I couldn't say. But there's something funny about the deal."

King waited.

"**DID YOU** ever," the Doctor went on, "hear of a genuine curse being appeased with money? What do gods or ancestors know about stocks and bonds? If James Waldorff had said that the curse would be appeased if the family brought back all the gold statues and trinkets and vases and things that were taken out of the temple, it would sound more logical. But we know that's impossible because they were melted up long years ago. But how ten million dollars left between a couple of pillars down there in the wilds could appease anybody but a human being who knows the value of money is more than I can figure out."

King smiled.

"It would seem," King said, "that you're coming around to believe that this is being done by some maniac who has developed a superhuman power over the dead."

"Confound it," the Doctor ranted, "you'll have me crazier than I am now. How do I know anything about it. I'm only spouting out things as they come into my head. Some things look very funny and others—"

He stopped short as King laid a hand on his arm, cautioning him to silence.

From behind came the distant roar of an airplane engine. King turned to him.

"Take a look out of the window. Tell me whether that plane is following this highway or just flying cross country."

The Doctor stuck his head out of the window, jerked it back suddenly.

"It is almost flat down on the road and is coming straight for us. I think—" he had to raise his voice to a shout—"it's going to crash us."

The drone of the engine was deafening. King was driving the light sedan at better than sixty. Suddenly he swerved to the side of the road and pushed down on the brakes. The car swerved and slowed.

Waaaam!

The plane leaped a few feet into the air, vaulted over the car and began to bank ahead of the car.

King stared at it with narrowed eyes. It was a small, open cockpit, two-seater plane. But it was fast. The cockpit in the rear was occupied by a head and shoulders in flying togs. The front cockpit was empty.

Instantly King shot the car into high. The speedometer ran to sixty—seventy—eighty and then hung between eighty-five and ninety.

"What you trying to do," yelled the Doctor, "beat an airplane with a car?"

King shook his head as he sat hunched over the wheel.

"No," he shouted back, "but if that plane has machine guns meant for us, they'll have a lot more fun aiming them at us at this speed than if we were going slower. I'll show you what I mean."

The plane had turned and was coming up the road behind them again. The Doctor watched it through the window.

"It's gaining," he yelled.

"Good," King snapped through clenched teeth.

He swerved to the right and clamped on his brakes. The car slowed. The plane shot over them and while it was doing that, King jammed the accelerator to the floor again.

"We've got to cover as much ground this way as we can," he explained. "If we can make that wooded section just before we turn into the bedrock drive, we can get clear while the ship is on a turn. I had this trick pulled on me once during the war while I was chasing a German staff car with a general in it."

The car shot up to eighty and the plane circled and came down again. Another swerve and a stop. Then the Doctor, who was leaning out of the window, shouted, "The pilot of that plane is waving."

"What?" demanded King.

"Must be someone who knows this car. Seems friendly."

They had just reached the wooded section of the highway. The trees, great tall ones, hung well over the road from either side so that they half hid the car as it tore along.

They flashed out into the open. King brought the car to a slow stop. The plane came down over them again. He didn't swerve this time.

"There," he said, "that ought to probe something. If that pilot had any shooting intentions, he had a swell shot that time. Now we'll try again and make absolutely sure."

The car came to a stop and King and the Doctor got out and ran to the front of it, stood there out in the open.

The plane had turned and was coming back. But the nose wasn't headed toward them. It was headed to the right. The ship was diving.

It roared past and the pilot waved. King frowned.

"That's funny," he said. "I'd swear I've seen that pilot before. Don't know any pilots in this part of the country. Maybe it's one from the Coast—but I don't know he'd track—"

The plane banked and came again. And as it passed even closer this time, the pilot waved them on.

"He wants us to go on," King said.

"Think it's all right to do so?" asked the Doctor.

King nodded. "We're going to chance it anyway."

They drove on, came to the turn that brought them into the secret hideout in the woods and drove down the bedrock trail. The plane circled above the trees. Then the engine slowed and could be heard to idle. It was descending over that field where King had his own fast six-passenger cabin plane staked down.

King broke into a run and reached the field in time to see the light plane coming down for a graceful landing.

His mouth dropped open as he saw a small pilot climb out of the cockpit, take off helmet and goggles, which revealed a mass of short bobbed hair. It was Constance Waldorff.

"I—I didn't know you flew," King gasped.

"I hope I haven't taken you too much by surprise," the girl said. "I had to come." She had a handbag in her hand, which by the way she carried it, seemed heavy. "You see, things have happened since you left."

"What," demanded King, "something else gone wrong? I thought just about everything had happened that could happen."

"Not quite," said Constance with a rather wicked gleam in her brown eyes. "There was one more thing that could happen. And it decided me to go with you to Yucatan."

She saw King glance at the heavy bag.

"No," she said in almost a whisper. "This isn't the ten million. It's sand. I found out I couldn't get anywhere near ten million. I didn't know what to do. I—I went into the library—to see if father—might be able to advise me."

Her under lip quivered.

"He was gone."

"Gone," exploded King and the Doctor at the same time.

She nodded.

"They were all gone," she said.

"You mean," the Doctor boomed, "that your uncle and your Cousin Henry, who was dead when I left him, and your father, were gone. All of them?"

The girl bit her lip.

"All of them gone," she said. "No one saw them. They apparently just vanished. So we're going to see this thing through together."

CHAPTER 12
POLICE PATROL

KING COULDN'T help but feel a surge of admiration for the girl as she stood there before him. She seemed so alone in the world, and yet so determined. She hadn't broken down in hysterical weeping as her cousin George had done. And yet with the exception of George, she was the only one left in the Waldorff family of whole body and sane mind.

King didn't hesitate when she said she was going along. He felt there was no use in arguing.

The Doctor was the first to speak. His heavy eyebrows lowered as he stared at the girl through slitted eyes.

"As I remember," he said, "there's only one door that opens into the library. That's the one from the main hall. Is that right?"

The girl nodded.

"That's correct," she said.

"Then, in that case," the Doctor pursued, "those three—that is your Cousin Henry, your father and your Uncle John, would have had to be carried into the front hall, where someone would probably have seen them."

"Yes," said Constance Waldorff.

"Was the butler around?"

The girl hesitated.

"I—I'm not sure," she said. "Poor Harvey, that's the butler, was so frightened that I don't think he'd remember anything if he did see it. I asked him and he stammered that he hadn't seen anyone. Then he asked me if I would relieve him from his duties."

"You let him go?" asked the Doctor.

"Of course, poor thing," she said. "After all, there's nothing he can do there, now."

King jerked his head toward the trees which hid the cabin.

"We can talk on our way to the cabin," he said. "I want to let the rest of the band know what has happened. Perhaps they have received some information over the short wave."

Constance Waldorff's eyes widened quickly.

"The Secret 6 certainly moves in a mysterious manner," she said. "What is this short wave you speak of?"

King smiled down at her beside him as they walked.

"It's not so wonderful as it might seem," he said. "The Doctor here is quite an expert on radio. He has designed small radios that can be plugged into an ordinary light socket and be used for sending messages short distances. We have given several of them to scouts who are working with us."

"How wonderful," said the girl. "And do they help you much?"

King nodded.

"In fact, on this case," he said, "I think we all might have swallowed the story of the Maya curse if it hadn't been for a warning from one of our scouts."

The girl's eyes widened.

"You don't believe in this Maya curse, then?" she asked.

"Except for two or three things, I don't know what to believe," King admitted. "That's why we're going down to Yucatan to investigate. But there's one thing that I am sure of. An ancient curse doesn't employ modern thugs to kill someone so that the curse can work better."

"You mean there are criminals trying to kill someone?" the girl asked. "Who, please?"

"I wouldn't worry about it," King smiled reassuringly. "But for your own curiosity, they're trying to kill me."

"Oh," said Constance Waldorff.

They reached the cabin and were greeted by the odor of cooking breakfast.

King pushed open the door, stepped aside for Miss Waldorff to enter.

Shakespeare, Luga, the Bishop and the Key blinked at the girl in riding breaches and leather jacket.

"Holy gee," the Key blurted out.

"Gentlemen," said King. "This is Miss Waldorff. She's come here to join us in a flight to Yucatan where the Maya curse is supposed to have its headquarters."

Shakespeare bowed with great dignity. The Bishop beamed.

"Welcome to our little jungle hideaway."

The Key grinned. Luga stood like an ebony statue. King thought he saw a look of fear cross Constance Waldorff's face as she sighted the giant black Zulu chieftain with his wild flying hair. He hastened to assure her.

"Luga makes a pretty fearsome looking character, Miss Waldorff," he said, "but you can feel safe while he's around."

"I certainly would hate to have him take a dislike to me," the girl said. "My, look at those muscles."

Luga stepped forward. He grinned broadly and bowed low.

"I go 'long on trip, Master," he said. "I take good care Miss Waldorff."

King nodded.

"I figured you'd go on the trip to Yucatan," he said. "That's a good idea, too, about taking care of Miss Waldorff."

"If you are flying down," the Doctor said, "you can count me out."

King smiled.

"I'm afraid we are going to fly, Doctor," King said. "And since you'd have a tough time dragging one foot all of the way to Yucatan, I guess that cuts you out of the picture."

"I think," said King. "The rest of us can go then. The Bishop, Shakespeare, Key, Luga, Miss Waldorff and myself. That will make a full plane anyway, Doctor."

"I don't care if the plane were empty," the Doctor boomed. "I have some things I want to check up on here. I'll rig up a radio on the ship so we can keep in touch with each other."

"Swell," said King. "Bishop, suppose you and Luga see about some provisions. Don't know how long we'll be down there."

"I'm so glad you're going by plane," the girl said. "That will give me a chance to help. I can fly part way—that is, if you'll trust me with the controls of your beautiful ship."

"After that landing I saw you make, Miss Waldorff," King said, "I think you could handle almost any plane."

"Suppose," cut in Shakespeare, "you tell us what has happened to prompt you to rush off to Yucatan."

King stopped short.

"That's right," he said. "Funny how I took for granted that you knew all about it."

"We got some dope from the Dummy," the Key put in. "That

guy knows his police if you ask me. He said there was a reporter that talked to the Indian, Manaha, and then after the reporter left, the police found the Indian gone. Got away through the grated window that was torn out by the roots. Then he said somethin' about John Flint comin' back to life and—"

"That's not half of it," said King. "The Doctor knows the story because he was with me. Suppose I tell you the rest when we get flying. Meantime, we've got to hurry with preparations."

The Bishop and Luga were hastily packing provisions for a stay of several days. The Doctor was assembling a radio set out of parts that went together under his seemingly clumsy fingers like clockworks at a jewelers touch.

Suddenly the room became electrified. Sounds were coming out of the short wave receiver.

"Pssst!" hissed the Key. "It's the Dummy again. Listen."

The words came clearer.

"No, it isn't the Dummy," the Key whispered. "It's the Worm."

"The Worm?" gasped Constance Waldorff.

King nodded and, stepping closer to her, whispered an explanation briefly in her ear.

"Hello, Secret 6," came the voice of the Worm. "Hello, Secret 6. Can you hear me? This is the Worm. Listen. I got some dope."

The room fairly throbbed with suspense.

"I was beggin' on a corner when my dog nuzzles a couple of guys. They jumps and turns around and I could see little wings they wore in their button holes. So I says to myself, there's a couple of aviators and they know what hard luck is. So I give 'em a story about gettin' shot down in the war and they hand me half a buck apiece. They pet the dog and then they stand close enough so I can hear what they're talkin' about."

"Seems the police think Constance Waldorff was kidnapped by The Secret 6 and they also got wind this mornin' about The Secret 6 takin' off to Yucatan in a plane. They have men watchin' at every airport and police planes is on the lookout. These two aviators was just leavin' their hotel to go out and fly around and see if they could spot the plane. The cops got an idea that the low-winged monoplane six-passenger cabin job that was brought up to College Point yesterday is for The Secret 6.

"Get me?" Wish there was some way you guys could let me know if you get all this stuff. Maybe you'll run into a trap if you don't get it. Maybe if you don't hear me, you should send me a post card. Ha-ha-ha."

THEN THE radio went dead. Members of The Secret 6 glanced at each other. Constance Waldorff was the first to speak.

"I'm afraid we'd better abandon the flight," she said," at least with me along. I don't want to get you men in any trouble."

King smiled.

"I don't think you need worry," he said. "But, of course, we don't want to force you to go."

"I want to go," the girl flared. "But I wouldn't place you in an embarrassing position for anything."

"I don't think you will," King said. "Are we all set?"

Heads nodded. They started one by one out of the cabin. The girl stayed beside him. She turned and spoke softly.

"I'd give a lot to know who called the police and told them that I was kidnapped by The Secret 6. I don't recall telling anyone

129

except—let me see. I did tell the butler, Harvey. I told him I was going to Yucatan with you and it was right after that that he asked if he might go. He seemed very nervous."

King stared at her.

"You don't suppose—" he began.

The girl shook her head.

"Harvey?" she said. "Heavens, no. He hasn't brains enough to figure anything like this out in the slightest detail. And he's really scared."

"But you say he left the house rather hurriedly?" King asked.

"Yes," she said. "He fairly ran out of the front door when I told him he could go. I don't know whether he'll ever be back."

"Probably not," said King. "I wish I'd thought of it before, but I don't suppose it will matter anyway."

The girl stared at him as they walked on.

"I'm afraid I don't quite understand," she said.

"Just the fact that you have that grip filled with sand instead of gold," King said. "If there is a man behind this, he'll be coming for that grip—" He glanced at her sharply. "You didn't tell anyone that it contained only sand?"

She shook her head. "Not a soul."

He nodded, took a map that he had stuffed into his pocket and began studying a course. They reached the plane and while the others were storing the provisions and the Doctor was installing the two-way radio set, King continued to study the course.

The girl looked over his shoulder.

"I think," he said, "that the police will expect us to take the shortest route. Down the coast to Florida and then to Cuba and then to Yucatan. So we'll fool them. We'll go to Brownville, Texas, which is on the Border and the Gulf of Mexico. But we won't stop. We'll go over the line into Mexico. There we ought to be safe from the United States authorities."

"But you'll have to stop somewhere between for gas," she prompted.

"Several times," said King. "With this load, we can't carry gas for more than eight or nine hundred miles. A thousand at the most. I think we have about an hour's gas right now. I believe I'll fly straight north across the Sound to New Haven. We should be able to gas up there for the first stretch without much danger as they won't be expecting us to go that way."

The six climbed into the cabin. Constance Waldorff sat in the front seat across from King before a pair of dual controls.

The Doctor waved. King taxied out and down the field. He turned into the wind, made sure the motor was warm enough, then gave her the gun. The big cabin plane shot ahead. And when they were cutting through the air, with the mufflers quieting the sound of the motors roar, he told the others what had happened. A little while later they landed at the New Haven airport where he ordered the tanks filled. The gas wagon drew up in front and gas began to flow. The tank was almost full when someone came running from the office door of the hangar.

"Just a moment, sir," the young man shouted. "I think there's a message coming through for you over the wire."

"How do you know my name?" demanded King.

The face of the man went a shade whiter.

131

"It—it's for the number of your ship, sir," he stammered.

"Good," said King. "We'll wait."

The man seemed relieved. He turned and trotted back. King spun on Constance Waldorff.

"See if you can see any other ships coming this way." Then to the gas man, he said, "That's enough. Pull out the hose and slap the cap on the tank. We're going."

Connie Waldorff jerked her head in for a moment.

"There's a plane coming from the east!"

Then she peered out again as King spun 'round in his seat and stared in that direction.

He saw little more than a speck in the eastern sky. But it was growing large rapidly. A fast ship, that. It looked to King from a distance like a Northrup, but he couldn't be sure. Constance turned to him excitedly.

"I think," she said, "it's that Northrup the police have added to their collection."

She glanced out again. The low-winged speed plane was much closer now. She nodded.

"Yes," she said. "I'm sure of it."

King's teeth clenched. The mechanic was screwing the cap on the wing tank. King flung him a bill to pay for the gas and yelled—"Clear!"

He put the starter flywheel in motion and the motor of his powerful six-place cabin job whirred. Constance Waldorff half rose from her seat.

"Don't you think," she asked, "the best thing to do is to stay here and tell the police that you're not kidnapping me? That will protect you and—"

King laid a hand on her arm.

"You can get out if you want to," he said. "But I think things will work out better if you stay with the ship. We of The Secret 6 will take our chances if you'll take yours. The police will stop us, anyway—if they can, of course—if you wish to go, we don't want you to feel that you are kidnapped."

A faint smile crossed the girl's face then

"How silly of you," she said. "But I really can't see how you're going to avoid the police. From the air they can riddle you with machine-gun bullets and—"

"Before they can really catch and hold us," King said, "they'll have to land. And when they land, we won't be at a disadvantage anymore. Just watch and see what happens."

Everyone on that low-winged cabin plane of The Secret 6 watched. The police ship was circling the field to land. King let his great motor warm and moved the throttle so that the motors picked up. Then he was taxiing along the ground very slowly, moving down to a place where a little cloud of dust whipped up in the gentle breeze.

There he turned so that the plane stood sidewise to the wind; he would now have to swing 'round in order to take off… a turn of 90 degrees.

There came the *kerwump* of the landing gear on the big Northrup plane. King watched it. Through its windows police officers in uniform were visible. And the snouts of machine guns.

Both planes were large, and due to the fact, the police ship couldn't taxi very close to the other.

"Jolly," exclaimed the Bishop," you're surely not going to sit here and let them come over and take us without an argument?"

"Not if I can help it," King smiled back. "I'm only waiting until I can get them at a disadvantage. When I give the signal, everybody duck and get as low between the seats as you can. It won't be long. Here come three of the cops now from the Northrup."

"I think there are only five in that plane," the girl said.

"Right," said King. "That's what I counted."

"They have machine guns leveled at us," ventured Shakespeare rather nervously.

"Right," said King, "but they're some distance away. Even with those machine guns, they can't shoot too straight when I throw up the smoke screen."

"Smoke screen?" several voices in the cabin shouted at the same time.

"Right," smiled King. "I think it will work. Wait until those three get a little farther from their Northrup. There. That's good. Now duck for cover, because there's going to be some shooting. Duck!"

At that instant, King opened the throttle of the low-winged speed demon of the air. The great engine whirred. He kicked hard on the rudder bar and the plane spun a quarter of the way around, until it was headed for the field into the wind.

"Jolly," shouted the Bishop," look at that cloud of dust we're blowing up behind us. I can't see the police plane now or the officers."

Tac—tac—tac!

"That doesn't stop you from hearing the guns," King grinned. "But I'll gamble they're just as apt to hit each other as they are us. I pulled a stunt like this down in Texas in the old barnstorming days when a sheriff tried to serve me with a paper to stop me flying over a poultry farm. The rancher claimed I scared his chickens so they wouldn't lay. But he was an old crank anyway."

The Secret 6 plane was tearing along the surface of the ground. The wings grew light and the plane lifted and tore into the air. King glanced back out of his window.

"They're coming," he said. "But we did hold them up for a minute until those three cops could get their bearings in the dust and find their plane. Now they're taking off, too."

King banked hard over and flashed out across the Sound, heading for Long Island and the open ocean beyond. Connie Waldorff was staring out of the window.

"They're gaining on us," she exclaimed. "We've got to go faster."

"Sorry," said King through tight lips.

He glanced out of his window, too. The police plane was gaining. Not rapidly, but it was coming up behind them. There could be no doubt of it. King reached up for a special lever over his head and pulled. A deafening roar blasted out. That lever cut out the muffler and allowed the exhaust fumes to escape direct into the air. There was no need of trying to muffle the sound of their motor now. They needed all the speed they could get.

They were hurtling over Long Island Sound at nearly two hundred miles an hour. King could glance down to the east and see the place where the hideout jungle of The Secret 6 was located. No doubt the Doctor was down there, watching them scream southward.

Connie Waldorff was still sitting beside him with her head out of the window slightly so that she could look back. The pressure of the driving wind from the giant propeller was terrific against the back of her head, but she seemed not to mind it.

"They're still gaining," she said. "Can't we go faster?"

King shook his head. His lips formed a hard straight line across his white teeth. He parted them long enough to say—

"I'm sorry. She's doing all she can."

CHAPTER 13
AN EMPTY COFFIN

THE DOCTOR had waved to his friends when The Secret 6 plane took the air. He shook his head as it turned north and vanished from sight.

"By George," he murmured, "I wish I had the nerve to fly in one of those things. There must be something about it—until you crash."

He turned then and returned to the cabin. There he took certain things from his laboratory in the loft of the cabin and went out.

He didn't bother to lock the doors. The cabin was so hidden in the trees that there was very little chance it would ever be found by anyone who wasn't looking for it.

He climbed into his own fast sedan and headed for New York.

He drove slowly, as though he had all the time in the world. For the Doctor wanted to spend some time thinking.

The traffic grew heavier and heavier. He crossed a bridge and then made his way toward Woodlawn cemetery. Once in the cemetery, he wound the circling drives slowly until he came to the vault where earlier that morning they had found James Waldorff, the living dead man, struggling to get out of the tomb.

He stopped his car before the vault and got out. Now in the daylight he could see things quite clearly. No one, apparently, had been at the tomb since James Waldorff had come out of it.

It gave him a strange feeling to be standing there now before that place in broad daylight. A few hours before it had seemed so horrible, so ghastly. In the daylight it seemed just another costly cemetery vault.

He studied the heavy grated doors. That night he had taken for granted that they were of heavy iron. But now he saw he had been mistaken. They were of the best and heaviest bronze.

He took out his magnifying glass and examined the marks about the keyhole. Then he remembered that almost everyone in the group had touched that door and parts of the grating. Henry Waldorff had touched it and his son George and Constance and even he, himself, when he helped King guide the living corpse out of the place.

That wouldn't do much good then. He shoved his magnifying glass into his pocket again with a grunt of disgust. The grated door that led into the vault was locked. He stared at it thoughtfully. He couldn't remember whether it had been locked by Henry Waldorff before they had left or not.

After a moment, he brought out a great ring of keys—large ones and small ones.

He tried several in the lock before he found one that fitted. Even so, he had to wiggle it about considerably before the bronze lock gave way. The gate swung open heavily.

Without the slightest hesitation, he went inside. The place smelled dank and musty as it had the night before, but not as strongly of mold.

"One thing sure," the Doctor said to himself, "I'm going to find out right now whether James Waldorff is a victim of Black and White Magic. He must have been lying in a casket and a mighty tight one, too. The condition of that casket should tell something about—"

He stopped short and stared. The whole interior of the vault was in stone and bronze; it was bisected by a corridor about fifteen feet long. Along each side a row of three shelves were placed. And the front of some of the shelves were sealed with marble slabs that were marked with names of the dead entombed behind them.

But the thing that caused the Doctor to stop and stare was one of those marble slabs that had covered a coffin on the second shelf. It had been pushed out, apparently from the inside, and was broken where it had landed on the floor.

On one of the pieces, he saw inscribed the name of James Waldorff.

Behind it stood a richly covered casket with solid silver handles and decorations.

The top was torn open, broken piece from piece, as though some great force from within had heaved upward and forced the lid off. He stepped over and bent down to examine it.

Once he had had occasion to exhume a body that had been buried for two or three months. It had been a bad mess. The inside of the casket had been moldy. The body had stunk of decayed flesh. And the face was covered with mold until it was beyond recognition.

But this was different. There was mold in this casket. But only in one place—where the head had laid. The rest of the silken lining had a damp, musty look.

"That," said the Doctor to himself, "is what I can't understand. It would seem that the head dies but the body lives on. And yet, if the head dies, how is it that the vocal chords are left?"

He shook his head, baffled.

Then he started examining the casket lid more closely. He puffed meditatively on a cigar as he stared at the ghastly picture.

"It certainly looks," he decided, "as though James Waldorff pushed his own way out of that casket."

He bent down and examined the screws that had held the lid on. Some of them were pulled out by the roots. Others had held and the metal and wood had been forced up around them.

"I can't figure any other way to it," he mused. "If someone on the outside had wanted to let him out, all they would have to do would be to unfasten those screws and take off the lid."

Suddenly a thought seized him. If this curse were real, every corpse in that tomb should be in the same condition that James Waldorff had been in.

The Doctor turned and inspected the several marble slabs that sealed the last resting place of other dead of the Waldorff family. HE FOUND one that seemed slightly loose. Years of weathering had loosened the cement in the cracks. The Doctor went to his car in front, got a strong tire tool and returned.

With that he pried at the slab until he could pull it out of place. The name on the slab read:

JOHN WALDORFF

"I should think if any of the Waldorff family was due to get the Maya curse, John Waldorff, Senior would," the Doctor ventured. "He helped to actually rob the place."

Suddenly his hand slipped and the slab dropped to the floor. His mouth dropped open. The marble didn't break!

Queer, that. The other marble slab had broken in several places. He shook his head and continued his examination.

He caught hold of the handle on the end of John Waldorff's casket and pulled the coffin hallway out. A smell of rotting flesh and mold came to him. But only for a short time. Then he was working with a screwdriver, unscrewing the coffin lid.

The top was in two sections. He unscrewed the section that was exposed, lifted the lid gingerly. The odor that came out almost choked him. He saw bones and mold inside. Bones and mold that one would expect to find in the casket of any man who had been buried for a number of years.

Quickly the Doctor replaced the cover and screwed down

the top. He pushed it back into place and heaved on the marble slab. Set that in place, leaning slightly so that it wouldn't fall.

"Phew!" he sighed. "Old John Waldorff really died. No joking about that. I'll be blessed if I can figure it out."

He half turned to glance at the still open casket of James Waldorff. Then his big heavy lower jaw dropped open.

"What a fool I am," he boomed deep down in his throat. "Here I come to see whether James Waldorff escaped by himself or with the help of some human being. I find his tomb opened and his casket out on the floor, apparently broken from the inside."

He shook his head with clenched teeth.

"But I came close to missing the easiest thing of all," he went on. "How could a man inside that casket pull it out of the niche and place it on the floor and then break it open?"

He growled angrily.

"Why, confound it," he snapped. "I ought to have someone kick me all around the block for almost missing that. There was someone else in this tomb before we found James Waldorff. Someone helped him out."

He whirled and inspected the opening out of which the marble slab had come. Now that he looked for them, he could see little marks in the broken marble and in the framework where it had fitted. Someone had pried that slab out of its place with a strong instrument, just as he had pried the slab of John Waldorff out with a tire iron.

"They must have thrown it on the floor several times to make it break like that," the Doctor continued.

He hurried to the open casket, turned over the broken lid and stared at it. Now he could make out the mark of some heavy weapon, like a crow bar, that had been inserted in one end to pry off the cover.

He gave a short, definite nod. Taking a piece of chalk from his pocket, he bent over the casket and drew a small insignia.

(0

And when he went out and re-locked the bronze gate with his skeleton key, he made another smaller mark on the lock plate.

As he climbed into his car, he said, "I've been a fool to think that this was Black Magic or a Maya curse. There is a human being behind it. I don't know how it is accomplished, but at least we know what we're up against. Human hands have done everything that has been done in this tomb."

Then the Doctor started the engine of his sedan and drove out of the cemetery.

CHAPTER 14
ESCAPE

KING AND his five passengers were heading across Long Island, tearing the air apart in their flight from the police plane. He turned to the girl beside him.

"You've been around some of the New York airports," he said. "Do you know anything about the equipment of that police plane?"

"You mean the motor?" she asked. "I think they've got a super Hornet."

King shook his head.

"I mean her guns. I've heard something about a one-pounder mounted on the wings. I'm wondering if this particular plane has such a thing. I saw a bulge on each wing just outside the propeller radius that looked suspiciously like it."

Connie Waldorff thought for a moment.

"I have heard something about police planes trying out a new gun," she said, "but I wouldn't be too sure."

King bit his lip.

"We'll know more about it before long when they get near enough to try it," he told her grimly.

They reached the south shore of Long Island and droned out over the open sea. He was flying entirely by compass now. Pushing back his window, he made a slight turn to the left and, at the same time, looked out.

As he brought his head back in, he felt Connie Waldorff's eyes upon him.

"They're gaining, aren't they," she asked softly.

King nodded. "I'll say they are," he said. "What luck that is. And the Northrup is the only thing I know of that could beat us in speed. They aren't making more than five miles an hour more than we are. They're about two miles behind yet. But figure out a five mile an hour gain and tell me how long it will take them to come within range of us—at least with that one-pounder."

"About fifteen minutes," the girl said instantly.

"I've thought of one thing," she continued after a minute.

143

"They think I'm here with you in this plane. Don't you think that might stop them from firing for fear they'd hit me?"

King considered for a long moment.

"I'm not so sure for several reasons," he said. "You've got your helmet and goggles on. If they did see you back at New Haven airport, they probably didn't recognize you. And anyway, I'm not so sure they'd miss a chance of getting The Secret 6, even though it endangered you."

Blllam!

The sound of a shuddering burst came to King and his passengers just as he finished. He whirled and peered back

"They sure are gaining," he said. "And that"—he shook his head— "was the bellow of a one-pounder, unless I'm crazy."

"But it sounded to the right side and behind," the girl said.

"I think," said King, "it's because your window is the only one in the cabin that's open. But the shot missed. That's one nice thing about those one-pounders. They blow up the minute the shell strikes anything—even something as slight as the slip stream of our prop."

Blllam!

Another explosion sounded, this time behind them.

King swerved the plane and glanced back again. Yes, that police ship was coming even faster than he had guessed the last time. The Bishop's voice cut in on his jumbled, racing thoughts.

"Remember the old saying," the Bishop yelled. "One to warn and the second to scare and the third…."

"When that comes," King shouted back, "we may not be here."

AS HE whirled, his eyes had caught sight of something ahead. Out across the ocean to the south, a layer of broken clouds hung low over the water.

He checked his altitude. Five thousand feet. Those clouds were a little higher. He pushed on the throttle to make sure that the engine was giving him all the power she had, then pulled the control back slightly. They were climbing. Climbing rapidly. If they could only reach that cloud bank, things might work out okay.

He moved his rudder back and forth to change course. He must dodge that next shot. It would come before many more seconds. He was sure of that. And they must not be there when the shot was fired. One direct hit was all that was needed to blast the plane and the six in it to eternity.

Blllam!

The sound of the shot came again and King knew that they had been missed.

He continued to climb and shift his course a little, constantly. Connie Waldorff glanced out of the window again on one of those turns.

"They're following, trying to keep their nose on you," she said.

"You mean trying to keep their sights on us," King corrected.

That elusive cloud bank seemed to be coming nearer, although it still was miles away. With astonishing speed, it swept at them. Funny how those clouds fooled you. About the time they were apparently far way, you'd come blasting into them.

Blllam!

The whole ship wobbled and shuddered. King grasped the

controls, tried to keep the plane from pitching and diving. He heard the girl cry out something in his ear.

"Are we hit?"

For the moment he was fighting so hard to keep the plane on an even keel and find out the truth of that question himself that he couldn't answer.

As he fought, he happened to stare down. There was nothing but open sea below. He couldn't sight land in any direction."

Gradually the ship came out and leveled. He shook his head at Connie Waldorff.

"I don't think we're hit," he said. "Motor acting O.K. and the ship responds to the controls. They must be using a time shell. Pleasant to have the police experimenting on you with a new invention, isn't it?"

She tried to smile back at him, but the effort was painful. Mist drifted by them. Then there came another shell.

Blllam!

"Missed!" yelled King as they plunged into the protecting gray and white of the cloud. "I'd like to bet my life against ten bucks that they don't get another shot at us—this morning anyway."

"Holy gee," the Key explained, "you mean the cops can't see us in this fog?"

"Not unless they have a lot of luck," King sang back. "I'm turning straight out to sea, due east. I don't think they'll expect us to go that way. Later on we'll swing back and hit Jersey."

"Somebody is apt to see you there, aren't they?" questioned the Bishop.

King smiled. "If we fly at fifteen thousand feet, they won't."

They tore on. For five minutes they flew due east through the cloud bank—that would mean fifteen miles farther out to sea. Then King reached up and pulled back the lever that forced the exhaust through the muffler again.

Any chance ship below wouldn't hear their exhaust now. They were traveling at ten thousand feet.

He made a turn southwest and droned on through the mist. Now he had nothing to do until they broke out into the clear again, but watch his blind-flying instruments.

He heard Connie Waldorff beside him.

"That was nice work, King," she said. It was given in the spirit of one aviator handing a compliment to another.

King smiled down at her.

"Thanks, Miss Waldorff."

"Please," the girl said, "that sounds so formal. The whole gang around Roosevelt Field call me Connie. I like that much better."

"Okay, Connie," grinned King. "But I still insist on saying thanks."

He turned then for a second and glanced at the other four in the cabin. The Bishop was sitting with head forward on his ample chest, snoozing now that the strain was over.

The Key was curled up in his seat, dozing. Shakespeare lolled, his head on the back of the seat and mouth wide open, snoring. He looked anything but the dignified old actor.

Luga was wide awake as usual. He stared at his master, then grinned, showing a great row of white teeth. King turned to the girl beside him.

"You're been under a terrible strain, Connie," he said. "Why don't you lean back and take a nap? You may need it later on."

The girl blinked her eyes.

"My eyes do burn," she acknowledged. "I'll try, though, on one condition. If when I wake up, you'll let me fly for a time and get some sleep yourself."

King nodded. "That's a bargain. I'll be ready to get some shut-eye by that time."

The girl smiled slightly and curled up beside him. She closed her eyes. He watched her. And soon he saw the slow rise and fall of her shoulders as sleep took possession of her.

TWENTY MINUTES after that they broke down out of the cloud bank. They were still over the sea but just ahead King could see the breakers on the shore of south Jersey.

Satisfied with his location, he stuck the nose into the air and began to climb once more. It began to get cool inside the cabin. The altimeter rose so that the needle pointed to fifteen thousand feet. The ship was still deep in the cloud bank, which ended at seven or eight thousand feet.

The weather got better for a time. Now and then they struck breaks in the clouds even at fifteen thousand feet, but almost at once they plunged into deeper mist once more.

An hour after Connie had fallen asleep, King began to drowse himself. He turned and caught Luga's eye, motioned him forward. The big black crowded his way up the narrow aisle between the seats.

"What you want, Master?"

"Did you happen to bring along any hot coffee?"

The black head nodded.

"Got jug," he said. He went to the rear of the cabin and returned with a gallon jug and a cup which he poured full of coffee.

King drank it down and nodded.

"Thanks," he said. "That's better."

He lighted a cigarette and smoked, took a look at his gasoline gauge. The gauge said the tank was half full. He checked his time. They'd need gas just about lunch time. He got out his map and tried to figure where they would be then.

Noon should find them somewhere over Tennessee. He began to wonder where they could find a place that would be safe to stop for gas and something to eat. Likely every airport anywhere near a route to Yucatan would be notified to watch for The Secret 6 plane.

He smoked one cigarette after another to help him keep awake as the hours of the morning passed. And as he thought, an idea came to him. There were plenty of fields throughout the country with a gasoline station and hot dog stand nearby merely for the road trade. One of these hayfields would do the trick.

Suddenly, he looked at the little light that burned constantly on the instrument board before him. It had been put there by the Doctor when he had installed the radio set in such a way that it would blink when there was a message being sent.

Instantly King clamped the ear-phones on his head and tensed. A series of dots and dashes were buzzing into his ears. And as he read the message, his pulse quickened. Here at least was the key to what they had been seeking:

Investigation at Waldorff vault proves that human hands opened James Waldorff's casket. Also have a tip from Legs Larkin. He was selling lead pencils this morning and heard that the fastest plane in the New York area had been chartered to fly south to Mexico. Let me know if you Kent any checks on this end. The Doctor.

The message was repeated to make sure that King received it. And this time he copied it down. That finished, he flipped his set over to sending and with the key, ticked off a message to the Doctor.

Escaped cops. Just got your message. Flying high somewhere over eastern U.S.A. Yucatan bound. Thanks. Let me know if anything else comes up. King.

As he finished sending that reply, the ship broke out into the clear, still at fifteen thousand. He glanced at his gas tank. The girl beside him stirred restlessly, then she sat up and blinked. She gave a start as she looked about her.

"Oh," she exclaimed. "I forgot where I was. Thought for a minute I'd been flying and had fallen asleep. Where are we?"

"We've been over New Jersey and Pennsylvania and Maryland and West Virginia and I think we're just over Kentucky now," King answered.

He saw the girl glance at the gas gauge.

"We'll have to stop for gas before long," she said. Then she noticed the slip of paper in his hand. She looked at it and King handed it to her. Her face grew troubled as she read it.

"But I can't figure out who might have done all this," she said.

"It must have been some jolt to the Doctor to learn this," said King. "He's stuck to the idea all along that it was the Maya curse or Black Magic."

He saw the girl bite her lip.

"You—you don't think that father could have anything to do with it," she asked. "After all, he was the one who told us to come down here."

King shook his head. "Don't worry, Connie, I haven't once had the slightest notion that it might be your father. It couldn't be. It's impossible."

"Everything is impossible," she murmured thickly.

"But I think we're on the way to clear up some things," King declared. "Perhaps everything. Did you notice the last part of that message? Someone is trailing us down here."

CHAPTER 15
DEAD MURDERER

THE GIRL'S eyes widened. "What makes you think that?" she demanded.

"As a matter of fact," King went on, "I planned this trip just so that the guilty one would follow us. Perhaps we can corner him."

"I wish I could feel certain of anything," said the girl.

"I think we will before many more days," King answered.

He glanced down over the side and in front, checked his map and the time and the gas gauge.

"We ought to be about over Tennessee right now," he guessed. "And our gas is getting low. We've got to pick a place pretty soon." He dropped the nose and went down to ten thousand, then to five. From here they could pick out fields. He crossed what looked like a good highway but little traveled. Here and there a car moved along like a snail.

Then he straightened. He had located a large pasture lot with three horses in one corner. And in the other, facing the highway, stood a gasoline station.

King dropped the nose again. He throttled back the engine and flew back and forth over the field twice to see if it was smooth.

Then he came down into the wind. The field was a bit rolly but he made a good landing. A man appeared at the corner of the gas station and a youngster ran toward them.

King taxied hurriedly toward the gas station, stopping the plane as near as he dared to go to the building. Then he kicked 'round into the wind, so that he would be ready to take off at a moment's notice.

He turned to the others, who had by now awakened.

"Might as well get out and stretch your legs while we're taking on gas," he advised.

He climbed out. The man from the gas station met him as he touched the ground. His eyes were wide.

"That's a mighty perddy plane you got there, mister," he said. "Ain't never had nobody land in that field since a flyin' circus come through 'bout eight or nine years ago. I always said that the Government ought to buy this field for emergency landin'. Why we got—"

"Be swell," King cut in. "Good field. We almost ran out of gas and had to come down."

"Well, say," said he man, "you're just in time. The tank wagon come this mornin' and filled me up for the next couple of weeks. I got my two hundred gallon tank full right up to the brim and the hundred gallon tank, she's full too."

King figured mentally for a moment.

"I'll take two hundred and fifty of that," he decided.

The lower jaw of the man dropped down on his chest.

"Huh?" he exploded.

King smiled. "Sure," he said. "These airplanes just eat up the gas."

"Well, I should think they did," the man agreed, still gaping. "But jumpin' Jehoshaphat, what am I goin' to tell my customers? I got my supply for the next ten days or two weeks, anyway."

"Gosh, what if my regular customers come and I ain't got no gas? I don't know."

"Couldn't you send the gasoline company a post card saying you need more gas?" King asked, trying to keep his face straight.

"Say, come to think of it, I guess I could do that," said the other.

"And could we get something to eat?"

"Eat?" repeated the man. "I was just goin' to lunch myself. Lucky you come when you did. I was just goin' to lock up the place and go down to the house. Hey, you, David—" he called to the youngster who was doing everything to inspect the plane but climb into the engine— "you run down and tell your ma to hurry up and bring what we got in the house to eat."

153

The boy left reluctantly. King touched the man on the shoulder.

"Let's get going with the gas," he suggested. "I've got a big funnel and a chamois to strain it through. You start pumping a can of gas and I'll get ready to pour it into the tank."

By some miracle of good luck the man finally got the idea that time was precious and shambled off to pump gas.

They worked with that five-gallon can until it seemed that half the afternoon would slip by before the tank was full. Now and then a passerby stopped and lingered. By the time the tank was full, it seemed that the whole county had heard about the plane and had come to see it.

"No time to stay here and eat," King told his passengers after he paid the bill. "We've got to shoe off before somebody comes along and recognizes the ship."

They all climbed back into the cabin. King had considerable shouting to do before the way was cleared about that great propeller. Then he started the engine, warmed it for a minute or two and waved to the crowd. As they took the air, Connie Waldorff said, "Remember your promise. It's my turn to fly now. Where do we go from here?"

King studied his map.

"Matamoros," he said. "That's just across the Rio Grande. Brownsville is the last airport on the United States side. And Matamoros is the first place across the border in Mexico. We can stop there for the night, I'm sure, without much worry about the police."

"And we have enough gas to reach it?" asked the girl.

"I think we have with the wind in our favor down here," King said. He checked his map again, figured a straight compass course and set the plane on that course. "Hold her with the compass there," he told Connie. "If you should get a little off your course, we'll know where we are when we hit either the Rio Grande or the Gulf of Mexico."

The girl took the controls. King slumped down in his seat and the gentle muffled throb of the great engine music to his ears, fell asleep.

HE JERKED upright hours later. Like Connie Waldorff, he couldn't realize immediately where he was. He glanced wildly about him, saw Connie smile, then he glanced down. Blue water was far below. "The Gulf of Mexico," Connie explained. "I hit it abut ten minutes ago and have been following the map down the coast toward the mouth of the Rio Grande."

King smiled at the girl.

"Nice work," he complimented. He glanced at the gas gauge, checked a town below on the map. "That is nice work," he said again. "We aren't much more than ten minutes out of Matamoros."

The flying had taken Connie Waldorff out of herself for the time being, made her forget in some measure, the ghastly incidents of the past hours. She smiled almost happily at him.

"Wouldn't it be more correct if you said that you timed your nap just right?" she ventured.

King took over the controls now and the girl gave them up willingly. They swept up the Rio Grande, could see Brownsville on the right bank of the river and Matamoros on the left.

155

King turned for the Mexican town just across the border.

A few minutes of circling showed him the airport there—a little field with a small building in one corner of it. And the field was marked with a semi-white circle in the middle.

He landed. A Mexican who spoke good English came out to meet the plane. King arranged for gasoline and oil and transportation into town, where they found a comfortable hotel. It was while they were leisurely eating dinner that night that the Key asked, "Say, listen. I been tryin' to figure somethin' out and I can't get it straight. That message we got from the Doc looks like it proves that there ain't any Maya curse. It's just a racket of some guy that's got a queer way of puttin' things over."

The others nodded and waited.

"Well, listen," the Key went on. "How do we know that this Maya servant didn't do the job?"

"I'm sure he hasn't anything to do with it," Connie Waldorff said instantly. "He's been with Uncle John ever since I was a little girl. I only saw him once and that was about ten years ago, but I know Uncle John would trust him with anything."

King leaned across the table toward the Key.

"Just what makes you think that Manaha had anything to do with it?" he asked.

"Huh?" said the Key. "Why, hel—I mean goodness, it's as plain as a Roman nose. Can't you see it?"

"I asked you for your reason," King reminded him.

"Well, in the first place, what happens the minute he escapes from jail? While he's in jail, nothin' happens. Right after you talk to him at the sub-station, he escapes and when you get to the morgue, there's Uncle John sittin' up on the marble slab. Then Uncle John disappears on the way to the hospital and you know the rest. And it all happened while the Indian was out of jail."

"All but one thing," King said. "Manaha couldn't have reached the morgue before I did if he'd been the best magician in the world. I'm sure he is not guilty."

"Yeah," said the Key. "Any guy that studies voodoo stuff and can slip stuff out of a safe right under the cops' noses, can get away with anything. Don't kid yourself about that."

Connie Waldorff turned then. "May I ask a question? I heard you talking about that safe of Uncle John's before, but I guess it didn't register clearly. Will you repeat it, please, King?"

"Gladly," said King. "That's one point I'd like to get cleared up in my own mind."

He stopped to light a cigarette. Went on.

"When we first went aboard the yacht and found your uncle's body, I saw the safe and just for luck, I turned the handle. It was unlocked. I found considerable cash inside in bills and a few stock and bond certificates of very large denominations."

"I didn't remember you told me that," said the girl. "I do remember you said that the police stated the safe was empty. Didn't you say the police boat chased you away from the yacht?"

"Right," said King. "And that's the queer part of it. I wouldn't suspect the police of robbing the safe. And no one put a foot on that boat from the time we left it until the police stopped there a minute later."

The girl frowned.

"But then what happened to the money?"

157

"That's what I'd like to know," King said. "Manaha was on the police boat and I have a hunch there was some other civilian, too. Just as the captain started to tell me his name, he was interrupted. I'd give a lot to know who the other civilian was."

The girl straightened. "I think I can answer that question," she said.

Every eye turned upon her.

"You can?" King exclaimed.

"Why, yes. But I can't see what difference it makes. Cousin Henry was with them."

"Cousin Henry?" echoed from at least three throats.

"**YOU SEE,**" the girl went on, "when Manaha told the police Uncle John was dying, they 'phoned our house. Cousin Henry happened to answer. He didn't tell me much—I suppose he didn't wish to frighten me. He just said there had been some trouble on Uncle John's yacht, and he was going to see about it. So he went with the police as a representative of the family."

The Key shrugged and pushed his chair back.

"Well, hel—"

"Ah, ah, ah," cut in the Bishop.

"Gee, I mean goodness," the Key grinned sheepishly. "What more can you ask? That's a cinch. Cousin Henry wanted the old guy's dough so he killed him, gave him some kind of poison that didn't work fast and then went out with the cops. I'll bet he made an excuse for being alone with his dead cousin and then robbed his safe and—"

The Key suddenly lost his nonchalance and became excited.

"Say, listen. I ain't such a bad detective. Listen. Now, this Cousin Henry didn't figure in the big fortune, is that right?"

King nodded patiently.

"Okay. So he decides to get what dough is in that safe. He finds out that the Indian knows the combination and is always on board. But he knows he's superstitious. So he gives Uncle John the slow-working poison—the old man was up at your house before he left for the yacht, wasn't he, Miss Waldorff?"

The girl nodded.

"Yes, he was," she said simply.

King shot a sidelong glance at her and frowned.

"Well, there you are, then," the Key hurried on triumphantly. "And he had a drink or somethin' up at your house, didn't he Miss Waldorff? Cousin Henry was there?"

"We were all there together," said Connie. "Uncle John had dinner with us that evening before he left for a cruise."

"It's a cinch," said the Key. "See how it works out? Henry knows that the Indian will tell when Uncle John dies. And he knows Uncle John is careless with the safe and maybe Henry Waldorff didn't have so much dough as you thought. So he comes along with the cops and gets a chance to be alone with his dear Cousin Henry and takes out the dough. You catch Cousin Henry and keep him out of circulation for a while and things are goin' to clear up like a rainstorm with a fleet of taxis in sight."

King nodded slowly. Very slowly.

"Sounds swell, Key," he said. "But you missed one thing. Henry died early this morning—of the same thing that John

Flint Waldorff died of. The Doctor felt his heart and pronounced him dead."

The Key's eyes bulged for a second. Then he said in utter disgust:

"Nuts. You guys ain't got any respect for a good story anyway."

Connie Waldorff pushed back her chair. "I think I'll retire," she said.

King waited until she had gone, then he lighted another cigarette.

"I'm going to see that the ship's staked down and then I'm going to turn in, too," he said. "Tomorrow's going to be another day—and what a day if my guess is anywhere near correct."

CHAPTER 16
THE TEMPLE OF AZRAH

KING WAS up at dawn. The others were about shortly after. Connie Waldorff came down to breakfast looking refreshed, but with a trace of dark circles under her eyes that showed all her sleeping hours hadn't been spent in sound slumber.

After a hasty breakfast, they went to the airport. The plane was ready. They climbed in and took the air.

There was little said that morning. Everyone seemed to have said all he could think of already. Particularly the Key.

One stop was made at noon at Mexico City for fuel and luncheon. There King got a more complete map of the area south, the Yucatan.

160

It was mid-afternoon when King, following that map with Connie Waldorff's help, spotted the lake her father had mentioned in his weird orders.

The lake was marked on the map and it was below them now in reality. Lake Grenla. It lay in the deep forest of the tropics. Moreover, it was hot and the air was rough over the hilly country.

From two thousand feet above, King circled in a wide area. He sighted the ancient Maya Temple of Azrah, looming through trees and jungle growth.

Coming down to a thousand feet, he could see the great pile of carved masonry more distinctly.

The lake was perhaps a mile north of the temple ruins.

He glanced at Connie. Her cheeks were flushed crimson with excitement.

"It seems hard to believe that all the horror that has taken place could have originated in such a peaceful spot," she said.

King tried to think of a reply. But couldn't. So he simply remained silent, cut the gun, raised the wheels and prepared to land.

Down, down they went. The water of Lake Grenla looked clear and free from snags that would rip the pontoon bottom. Lower and lower. Then there was a gentle swish of water and spray and they were down.

They were taxiing toward the south shore nearest the temple. Suddenly Luga called out a warning. King whirled in his seat. He saw the giant black man pointing to the west bank.

"Master. Look. Somebody move. See?"

King spun 'round and tried to see.

"Too late," said Luga sadly. "Gone now."

"What did it look like, Luga?" King asked.

"Luga not see very good," came the answer. "Look like somebody in bushes looking at us. They go back out of sight."

"Most likely it's a Maya Indian," said Connie. "My grandfather used to tell me about them when I was a little girl. He said they were a harmless people. He liked them. I think he did as much for them in finding that Temple of Azrah as he did for his own family. He gave all of the Indians that helped him enough money to live on the rest of their lives and he built a school for their children in Izamal. That's the nearest town to this temple."

King frowned. "You mean your grandfather was that considerate and still the Maya curse is supposed to have killed several of his family?"

"It doesn't seem reasonable," said the girl, "does it?"

"It certainly does not," King returned emphatically.

They had reached shore by this time. King climbed out first. Made the plane fast to trees with rope, then he helped the others descend to the tangled bank.

It was Luga who took command now. He led the way through the jungle to the temple. And that mile walk was a struggle, even with the giant black beating down the tangled growth so that those who followed might do so more easily.

Everyone but Connie carried his share of the supplies and ammunition. She carried her leather bag of sand. And every member of the party carried a loaded gun.

The party came upon the Temple Azrah completely by surprise. The brush had grown thickly about it. So thickly that they did not see it until they burst through a thicket and almost walked into the ancient walls.

They were looking upon what seemed to be a corner column. It sloped backward and the face of it was carved with images of the picture writing area.

"I think," said King, "we might as well go on until we come to the main entrance."

Luga turned along the wall. The tower was set out from the corner of the great stone edifice on both sides and sloped back almost gradually enough to be climbed. But not quite. The main walls were cut back on each side of that corner tower and ran straight up for twenty feet or so to the top, which was flat.

THE GIANT black looked back every few steps to make sure that Connie Waldorff was behind him. She followed closely, carrying her leather bag. Behind her came King and then the Key, Shakespeare and, last, the Bishop who was puffing slightly as he plowed through the tangled growth.

The wall that they walked beside extended some three hundred feet toward the west. The afternoon was growing late, and the thickness of the branches over their heads made a semi-darkness about them.

They pushed on through the thicket, came to another corner tower. It was similar to the first but the underbrush was grown so thick about it that they had to pull the bushes away to see the picture writing on its sloping walls.

"The entrance must be on the other side," King ventured. "We'll keep on until we find it."

Again Luga lead the way around the square, slanting tower and down another straight wall.

Now and then they broke out into open spaces that showed them daylight was still apparent above the leafy bows. Then again they plunged into the darkened aisles beneath the foliage.

A few minutes later they reached a third slanting tower. But here King and the others noticed something slightly different. The far side was chiseled much more elaborately than any of the others.

"I think," King said, "we've come to the front wall. We should strike the entrance pretty soon. Let's go.

Suddenly they broke through a particularly tangled mass of underbrush and there before them was a small clearing, perhaps fifty feet in each direction. But it was the Temple of Azrah that drew their attention.

The entrance was a pretentious affair. Four stone steps with ragged grass growing at either side dropped down to a massive stone door that was open wide enough for a big man to enter easily.

The stone work about the door was heavy chiseled with weathered images. A gigantic stone cut in the characteristic architecture of the Maya temples supported the roof and was in turn supported by two great carved pillars on each side.

King pointed to those pillars.

"I imagine," he said to Connie Waldorff," that those are the pillars your father mentioned."

"Yes," the girl nodded in an awed voice.

Suddenly Luga tensed and stood motionless like a wild stag

sniffing the air. King, catching a glimpse of him out of the corner of his eye, turned quickly.

"What is it, Luga?" he hissed.

The big Zulu chief shook his head, stood still. Everyone else froze in their tracks. Not a man moved. One minute passed. Then another. At the end of the third minute, Luga relaxed and stepped beside King. The others gathered closely about.

"Think somebody else here," said Luga. "Luga think he hear sound somewhere. No sound come when we stop. Somebody maybe hide and watch us."

King nodded. "That's about what I expected," he whispered back. "Have you any idea whether that someone is hiding in the temple or in the jungle?"

Luga considered for some time, then he shook his great head so that the wild black hair trembled.

"Not know, Master," he said. "Maybe they behind us in jungle. Maybe they in temple. Luga can't tell."

King hesitated for an instant before turning to the other members of the party.

"Keep your pistols and revolvers ready for instant action," he whispered. He turned to Connie Waldorff and, as he spoke to her, he raised his voice so that anyone within a hundred feet could hear.

"I think the next thing to do is to leave that bag with the ten million dollars in it between the pillars, as your father directed."

The girl's face was slightly pale. But she nodded and walked straight to the place her father had mentioned. Then, stooping, she set down the leather bag. King and the others were close behind her.

King had made a careful inspection of the surrounding thicket. Now he peered through the door into the darkened temple interior. Could see little. And again he spoke in a slightly louder than normal voice.

"I think while we're here," he said, "we may as well see the inside of this famous temple. Let's hope that the Maya curse will stop."

As he moved, he felt a hand on his arm. Turning, he saw Shakespeare.

"Might I suggest," said the old actor, "that gases are very apt to be present in any ancient tombs and temples. I have read of explorers being suffocated when they entered a place such as this."

"I think," King said, "that those cases are confined to tombs or a temple that has been sealed for thousands of years. But for the last fifty years or more at least this temple has been open."

"It might be well," the Bishop twinkled, "if we didn't transgress too far within these portals until we are sure what is inside."

"Right," said King. "I figure we'll just slip inside this door one by one and first get our eyes accustomed to the darker light inside. I don't believe any gases could possibly reach us if we go no further from the door than fifteen or twenty feet. The air is bound to circulate at least that far."

He entered first. The others followed, one by one.

AT FIRST they could see little except the floor and empty, chiseled pedestals. But as their eyes became accustomed to the dim light, they made out the entire interior of the gigantic temple.

It was a marvel of stone construction. Great pillars held up gigantic stones that formed the ceiling. Here and there at the sides of the great edifice, were arches. And there were many pedestals where the golden images that had formed the basis for the Waldorff fortune had probably once stood.

"Jolly," exclaimed the Bishop. "The place rivals our finest cathedrals."

King turned to Connie with a frown.

"I can well believe that there would be many bats inside here, as your father mentioned," he said. "But isn't it strange that we don't see any?"

He blinked for a moment to make his eyes more accustomed to the darkness, opened them again. He could see even more clearly now. Yes, the light that showed through the partially open door was certainly weird and ghastly.

He walked a little farther into the interior, took a deep breath to test the air. It smelled damp and musty, but otherwise, there was nothing strange about it.

At a sudden thought, he turned to Luga.

"Listen, Luga," he ordered, "if anything should happen while we're in here, you take Connie and get out through that door first. The rest of us will try to take care of ourselves."

The big black giant nodded.

"Yes, Master," he promised.

The Key came silently to King's side.

"Say, listen," he hissed. "What's the idea of what you said

outside about leavin' the dough and then beatin' it away and hope that the curse is goin' to get satisfied. You ain't goin' to do that, are you?"

King whispered an answer back at the Key. The others gathered tightly about him as he spoke softly.

"Not on your life," King said. "We came down here to get the human being who is behind this. The gods of the Mayas wouldn't have any use for money even if it was in gold coin. We're going to take a longer look around this temple to make sure no one is hiding there, then we'll leave.

"Here's my plan. I'll go back to the plane. Luga and the rest of you will swing around through the jungle and return here. You'll hide in the thicket opposite the door. When anyone comes to get that bag, you'll jump out and collar them.

"It is likely that no one will come for the bag until they hear our plane take off. I'll do that. Connie, you can go with me or come back here with the others and be in at the finish."

"I think I'll stay," the girl said firmly.

"Okay," said King. "Then I'll fly off alone. I'll come back in about two hours and find out what's been going on."

"It be dark then," Luga ventured.

"Almost dark," King corrected. "Is that satisfactory?"

Heads nodded. King turned toward the interior of the temple once more and moved a few more steps. Suddenly he stopped and stared. At the same time, he felt Luga's great hand on his arm.

"Master," hissed Luga. "Look. What that?"

King was already staring at a strange thing. Everyone saw it now. Perched on top of a pedestal far in the interior was a giant bat. It was half again as tall as a man. It's wings were half spread, ready to fly. And its great beady eyes were glowing.

But it was the face of that winged thing that struck horror to the six. The face of that bat seemed almost human.

Then the thing moved from its perch. It leaned out and the wings stretched to the sides. It left the pedestal and came floating toward them, across the vaulted roof.

The great feet were outstretched—feet large enough to crush a man if they could grasp him.

SHAKESPEARE LOST all his dignity and, turning to flee, tripped on a stone of the floor and fell. The Bishop stumbled over him and went down on his hands and knees.

King whirled as the beast came. He half carried, half pushed Connie Waldorff toward the entrance. Luga was beside him. The giant black didn't wait for more orders. He had enough. His job was to protect the girl.

He reached down instantly, picked her up in his arms and raced for the open door.

But that was what made King's blood run cold. The door was closing—slowly—slowly. Closing as though some unseen power was pushing it shut with ponderous motion.

The Key had stopped to help the Bishop and Shakespeare to their feet. King spun 'round. He couldn't go and leave those three loyal members of The Secret 6 behind him.

Luga and Connie slipped through the door just an instant before the opening grew too small. The crack was narrowing to eighteen inches. To a foot. To six inches.

King whirled to aid those on the floor. The Bishop and Shakespeare were getting to their feet.

Blam!

The walls echoed with the blast of a revolver.

The Key was firing straight at the monster that was only inches away now. The monster that they could see but dimly because of the growing darkness.

King caught a glimpse of it before he heard the massive door close with a heavy thud, leaving them in total blackness.

He aimed his gun at the place where the giant bat had been. The flame showed the monster knocking the Bishop and Shakespeare down with its wings.

Quickly, he emptied his gun. But in the last flash of flame, the bat seemed to be in as good condition as before. The final glimpse King got, the monster was settling over the fallen bodies of the Bishop and Shakespeare. Key was hurling lead into the carcass from the side.

"Hey, what the hell," the Key yelled. And the Bishop was not interested enough to correct his speech.

The voice of the Key echoed hollowly against the vaulted ceiling. King leaped to his side. And as he moved, he fumbled for his flashlight. In his hurry, he couldn't seem to find it. The hook on the flashlight caught in his pocket. He didn't know what minute that giant bat would see him through the darkness and leap to strike.

Then he got the flashlight out and pressed the switch. The interior of the temple was crossed with its beam. He swung it instantly to the place where he remembered the bat had been.

Something strange, almost unbelievable, was going on there. At the last flash of his gun, the flame had revealed the bat fighting the Bishop and Shakespeare, beating them with its great wings.

But now the bat was still. It was lying on top of the two men who were struggling to get out from under it. And the Key was tearing at the left wing of the bat—tearing it apart. Tearing the hide from the bony framework as though he had gone mad.

He cursed merrily as he tore. The Bishop got partially free. King helped him to his feet and leaped around to the other side of the monster to help Shakespeare get out.

"Ah, ah, ah," exclaimed the Bishop. "What language, Key. But I must say in this instance, your cursing is—well, perhaps, forgivable."

Then for the first time King, himself, touched the side of the bat. The surprise almost made him draw back. His hand came in contact with tightly drawn paper darkened to look like skin and hair in the dim light.

Straightening, he played his flashlight about the monster thing, inspected the hideous face, part man, part bat.

"Well, what do you think of your Maya curse?" the Key rasped, panting. "A hunk of paper, some pipes, paint and a false face.

"So that's it." King snapped.

"Sure," said the Key, tearing off more of the paper. "Look at this. The framework of the damn—I mean darn thing—is pipe or metal tubing. It's got joints and wings that move and—"

King was climbing up the framework. His hand struck a wire that extended up to the roof of the temple.

171

"Somebody," he said, "has been working this with wires and pulleys. Those wires go up to the ceiling and then—"

He flashed his light across the ceiling, ran it on over toward the door. The light wavered.

"Jolly," said the Bishop. But his voice came to King from far off and it was weak and unnatural. Somehow that light in his hand wouldn't work so well. He couldn't hold still.

He remembered seeing the Key try to clutch for support. The Key was staggering like a drunken man. He was falling.

The light went out. Total darkness. King tried to raise strength enough to press the button again. He managed to get another flicker out of the flashlight.

And in that flash he saw something else. The Bishop and Shakespeare were on their knees, swaying dizzily.

King caught himself before he fell. He leaned against the framework of the manmade bat, clutched the metal tubing that formed the frame, and tried to hold on.

He was on his knees. The blackness about him was spinning faster. Things were growing very dim. He couldn't think. Then everything went blank and the blackness of unconsciousness smothered him like a blanket.

CHAPTER 17
MAYA VENGEANCE

WHEN CONNIE WALDORFF first saw that giant bat flit across the temple, her feet froze to the floor. Then she felt King pushing her. The next thing she knew she was being picked up in the gigantic arms of Luga and carried headlong for the closing door.

She fought to stay inside. Something within her rebelled at leaving King and the rest in the temple. She pounded the great black chief on the chest with her tiny fists. But it made no impression.

Then they were squeezing through the door, and were outside. Luga leaped up the steps to the ground above. Connie found herself still pounding him.

"Don't take me out!" she cried. "I want to stay. Leave me—"

She stopped short with a sickly feeling. For she heard the grating thud of the door as it closed, sealing the rest inside that ancient temple.

Luga spoke.

"Luga sorry," he said. "Master King give orders. I do what he say."

Then he set the girl down on the stone paving. She turned and stared at him for a moment. Her eyes blazed with anger. Luga bowed with a sad expression in his dark eyes.

"Luga sorry," he repeated. "But Miss Waldorff not stay in there. Can do no good."

The girl stared up at the Zulu chief for a moment. Then the anger left her face and she nodded.

"I suppose that's true," she admitted. "But what can we do? The door is shut. We've got to save them. They'll—they'll die in there."

"Luga try to get door open," said the black.

173

He left the girl and went down the four steps to the great door.

Putting his shoulder against it, he braced himself and his muscles bulged. The girl watched him with her heart pounding. A surge of thrilling admiration rose within her as she saw those great muscles work and strain. But the door remained as solid as though it had been there for centuries. It didn't budge.

Luga tried and tried again. The sweat rolled down over his neck and back and shoulders, making him look like a gleaming statue in ebony.

Suddenly, Connie heard a sound behind her. She turned. A muffled scream left her lips.

She didn't have time to count the men in that party. They were dark bronze color, rather short and stocky, and powerfully built. She recognized them instantly from her grandfather's description as Mayan Indians. Indians that were stalking her without a sound.

At her scream, Luga whirled. A wild light of battle flashed in his dark eyes.

The Indians had crept as close to Connie Waldorff as Luga was to her himself. A wild rush and they clutched her. At the same instant, Luga leaped up those steps in one long jump. He tried to head them off but was too late for that.

Nevertheless, he went into action. A bellowing, blood-curdling cry left his lips.

"Kii—Hoo! Kii—Hoo!"

It was the old battle cry of the Amakozi tribe of the Zulus. He forgot for the moment that he had a loaded gun stuck in his trousers. This was a fight and Luga reverted instantly to the savage. He was a wild hand-to-hand fighting man.

True, he snatched his gun—but only as a club.

Indians swarmed about him. They came now from every corner of the clearing. Some of them were carrying off Connie. Luga was knocking others down right and left, cutting his way to the girl.

"*Kii—Hoo! Kii—Hoo!*"

He clubbed Indian skulls until there was no gun left in his hand. Then he seized a human body—the body of one of the larger Indians—and spinning it about, used him for a club.

There was one scream of pain from that Indian. Then he fell silent, for his skull was crushed in by the first gigantic blow as he hurled against three other Indians.

The Mayas themselves were armed with knives and clubs. But these flew from their hands as they tumbled before that terrible onslaught of the giant black man.

He whirled that human cudgel about his head until he had battered his way to the half dozen who were carrying the kicking, scratching Connie Waldorff toward the jungle brush.

Then he dropped it and rushed in closer. He seized the neck of an Indian in each hand. They were flung back and there was a sharp crack as the neck of one broke. Then another crack and both bodies fell to the ground, limp and trembling.

All that happened in the wink of an eye. Luga leaped ahead, battering with flying fists to get at Connie Waldorff and tear her from the grasp that held her.

He seized two more and cracked their necks. He was in the

midst of the Indians now. Every one was trying to get a knife in his back or a club on his head. But they didn't dare move too close, for Luga was fighting and whirling about so that he could see behind him and on all sides at almost the same time.

He had almost reached Connie. He saw her half turn and look back at him. She was fighting like mad to get free, but the Indians had her arms pinned and she could do little. Then she screamed and cried out in warning:

"Look out. Behind you."

Luga whirled. But the odds were against him. Three Indians dived in at him from three different sides. He merely caught sight of a larger man behind, swinging a great club.

Wam!

Luga felt the blow on the side of his head. He had ducked just a little. But not enough. Stars blinked at him in the lowering afternoon light.

Connie saw him stagger. Screamed again as that great club descended a second time and connected squarely on the skull of Luga.

Luga sagged. Went down in a heap and Indians swarmed about him.

CONNIE WALDORFF was being rushed through the jungle. The Indians were still carrying her. Everything seemed finished. King and those of his Secret 6 who had come on the trip, were locked in the temple. Luga was probably killed. And she, Connie, was being carried to some horrible destination.

The Indians were making good time. None of them spoke. No

word had been uttered since the swift attack except that weird blood-curdling battle cry of the Amakozi tribe.

Two Mayas were carrying her now. One had hold of her shoulder. The other held her feet. They went on and on. It seemed to be getting dark. She looked up through the tree tops, sure it was still daylight above.

Once she asked, "Do any of you speak English?"

The Indians didn't even shake their heads. One grunted. That was all.

An hour of fast traveling through that heavy jungle. She couldn't help but marvel how the Indians circled the heavier growths so that they did not have to plow through the thickest jungle. Probably this was a trail.

Without any warning, they broke out into a small clearing. There were huts and more Indians. Women and children gawked at the procession as it passed through what served as the main street of the village.

The procession stopped in front of the largest hut. An Indian with a wrinkled face and a strong physique came out and gutturaled something to the others.

He glared at her. But outside of that, his face was expressionless.

"Can you speak English?" Connie demanded as her two bearers raised her to her feet. She decided he was the chief.

He nodded. "Yes. Speak English," he said. "You want to know why we bring you here?"

Connie glared back at him. Something about him angered her.

"I certainly would like to know," she declared. "My grandfather was named John Waldorff. My name is Waldorff. Constance Waldorff. Perhaps you knew my grandfather. He was a good man."

The chief grunted and nodded.

"Good," he said. "We bring for get even. You call vengeance."

"Look here," cried Connie. "My grandfather never harmed any of you. He gave you plenty of money and built schools for your children. He—"

"Ugh," grunted the chief. "My father tell me about John Waldorff. We not hate him. We hate other Waldorff."

Connie's eyes narrowed.

"Would you mind telling me just what Waldorff you're talking about?" she flared.

"Three years ago man named Waldorff come here," said the chief. "We help him dig for more gold. He not find gold. Find something else—three vases. Have liquid inside. He not know what is. Try some on my people."

The chief broke off and beat his chest with his right fist.

"Try some on me," he said angrily. "I drink. Kill me."

Connie Waldorff's eyes widened.

"Killed you?" she gasped.

"Kill me. My people tell me. Then he give me something else out of other vase. My people say I come back. Say I walk around with face on chest. Give me drink from third vase. I come back to life. Other men my tribe not so good. My brother still look—" He motioned toward the edge of the village.

"Come. I show you."

He started off and Connie followed, surrounded by the Indians who had brought her there.

While she walked, she tried to straighten things in her mind. Which one of her relatives could have done this thing? John Flint Waldorff had made trips to Yucatan. Her father had come down now and then. And Henry had come down, too. But these, all of them, had fallen before the scourge of what was supposed to be the Maya curse.

She thought of her Cousin George. Perhaps he?

She shook her head. That didn't make sense either. And yet, he was the only one who hadn't been struck dead with the strange menace.

They reached a space at the edge of the huts. The chief stopped. It was almost dark but she could see quite plainly.

There before her was a ghastly sight. It seemed to be the burial ground of the Indian village. There were platforms on stilts. And on those platforms were bodies exposed to the weather and lashed down. She glanced up into the sky and saw buzzards wheeling overhead.

The chief noticed her glance upward. He nodded.

"Only my tribe, Maya Indians, do this with dead," he said. "It is best. Buzzards eat them. But buzzards not eat those. Circle all time for three years. Not come down. Maybe they know they not dead."

He pointed then beyond the cemetery to half a dozen weird figures that were digging in the earth with worn flat sticks. But the ghastly part of it was that they moved more like machines

Luba clubbed Indian skulls until there was no gun left in

his hand in his mad effort to rescue the girl.

than human beings. And their heads were bowed down on their chests like the heads of her Uncle John and of her father.

"My brother there," growled the chief. "He not made well like me. Men there only half alive."

Connie Waldorff stared in horror. Things were clearing up in her spinning brain. But as yet she couldn't think of anyone in her family who would be guilty of such a crime.

"What are they digging for?" she heard herself asking.

"They dig forever," said the chief. "We go out and feed, keep alive. They keep digging. Think they look for water that make well."

The girl shuddered. The chief turned, started back toward his hut. The guards pushed her after him.

"You come," he grunted. "Make ready for sacrifice."

TWICE ON the way back Connie opened her mouth to speak. Then she closed it again. They reached the chiefs hut and stopped.

"Do you mean," Connie asked in a voice that wasn't any too steady, "that you plan to make a human sacrifice of me?"

The chief grunted and nodded.

"Get even. You Waldorff. We kill you for what other Waldorff do."

"What did this other Waldorff man look like?" Connie asked suddenly.

"Big man. Tall," the chief answered.

That only made Connie's brain spin faster. That description would fit her father or her uncle or either of her cousins. The men of the Waldorff family were certainly big compared with these thick-set Mayas.

"You come. We start ceremony," said the chief.

Two Indians were rolling a log in the open space before the chiefs hut. When they turned, she saw it was hollow.

Behind it stood a heavy post, buried in fresh earth. The Indians began pounding on the log with their hands, producing a nerve-shattering, rhythmic beat. She shuddered.

Two of the guards seized her at a sign from the chief. They half carried, half dragged her toward the post. The whole village was coming from every direction. Not a word was spoken. Every member of that Maya Indian tribe seemed to know exactly what was coming.

The two guards who brought her to the post held her back against it while others lashed her body to it with thongs of leather and pieces of crude rope.

Her head throbbed with the death beat of that hollow log drum. There seemed nothing that she could do. It was almost dark. Every face in that circle was turned upon her. But not one, not even a female face, was friendly.

The drumming increased in tempo. The men began dancing slowly around the post to which she was tied. It made her think of the old Western movies featuring an Indian war dance. But this was more weird and slower. It was the death dance.

Every now and then one of the men dancers would swing closer to Connie and toss a dried twig at her feet. Before that dance was finished, she knew that there would be a great heap of tinder dry fuel. She could only think of one thing. She closed her eyes in a fervent prayer.

"God," she breathed. "Is it right that I have to suffer for what someone in my family has done? Haven't I suffered enough already? Please help King—and the rest."

CHAPTER 18
JUNGLE DEATH

LUGA'S FIRST realization of consciousness was the throbbing of his head. It came as though in a dream, as though some great machine were grinding his brain to bits. *Throb—throb—throb!*

He couldn't think clearly. He only knew that his head ached terrifically. Slowly consciousness came back to him. He stirred restlessly on the ground where he had been felled by the second blow of the club.

Suddenly he was sitting bolt upright. He was still in the clearing before the temple. The minute he opened his eyes, everything came back to him. Dead Maya Indians lay about him.

He leaped to his feet, now knowing that he had been lying there unconscious for almost an hour. It seemed to him that blow had been struck only in the last few seconds.

Hurriedly, he traced the tracks of Connie's captors. On the rocky paving before the entrance to the Temple of Azrah, it was difficult. But he remembered the way they had been headed when the light ended. He went to the edge of the pavement and searched the jungle beyond, found the prints of the Indian's feet here and there in soft earth and started off at a dog trot to follow.

Fifteen steps were covered swiftly by the giant black. Then as his mind awakened more keenly and his memory cleared, the thought of King and the Bishop and the Key and Shakespeare came to him.

They were there in that temple. He had tried to keep the Maya Indians from capturing Connie Waldorff. Had failed.

He turned instantly and retraced his steps. It was getting dark, but the clearing was light enough to see easily. He strode to the door of the temple. It was still closed tightly. He studied it now. Luga was no longer the sage he had been in the light; he was going about things more sanely.

That door swung from a great slit in the stone wall. The black chief inspected it. Now that he was taking the time to study it, he saw that it was a solid slab of rock nearly two feet thick and was hinged by part of the top and bottom being cut away to a roundish knob or axle.

The door seemed to extend beyond that for a considerable distance. Because of the darkness and the narrowness of the crack, he couldn't tell just how far.

He tried with his mechanical mind to work at figuring how that portal could be moved. He was satisfied that some human power had closed it. But how, when he, with all his strength, could not budge it?

He mounted the four wide steps, went past the pillars and around to the side wall, which he inspected.

None of the stones moved.

He left it presently and returned to the entrance. There was earth on one side of the carvings.

He leaped forward to examine it. Yes, there was fresh dirt there, little more than two or three hours old. Then he saw more dirt higher up and suddenly the full importance of it struck him.

Rising up the side of these carvings opposite the columns were small, narrow steps.

Instantly Luga was climbing like a monkey. Up, up he went, to the flat roof.

He reached it and stared about. It reminded him of a great raised square paved with large stones. He glanced more closely to the portion of it nearest him, then suddenly he sprang forward.

Near the edge of the roof was a hole about three feet square. A stone had been lifted from it. A flat stone that fitted exactly into the opening.

Luga peered down the opening into the darkened interior of a large, triangle shaped room. It was empty as far as he could see. But something at one side caught his eye.

He dropped down the opening. The ceiling was little more than six feet high, and he had to stoop as he walked to the thing that had attracted his attention. It was a huge, long stone handle perhaps twenty feet long and almost a foot in thickness. He worked along it toward the end that was fastened to a flat, door-like stone near the entrance of the temple. Then he knew the answer.

The door was moved by men pushing on that great stone handle. He leaped behind it and began to push. Nothing happened. He pushed with all his might, braced his feet against the rear wall and strained. Still nothing happened.

HIS BLACK brow wrinkled in furrows and he frowned in bafflement. There was some secret to opening that door that he did not know. He studied the walls. On the inner one, some distance from where he stood, he noticed something.

He stepped over to it, and touched wires pulled through an opening. Near it was another hole large enough for a man to look through; it opened on the inside of the temple. Luga peered through, but saw only darkness.

"Master!" he called.

No answer. He called again without any reply except the echo of his own voice. At a loss what to do next, he pulled the wires. There was a clanking sound; it was the metal framework of the bat being raised and lowered to the floor, but he didn't know that.

He rushed back to the great stone room, pushed on it. It didn't move.

He suddenly knew that he was baffled. Dejected. His head throbbed unmercifully from his recent efforts. The stone lever was about waist-high. He leaned on it for a moment to rest himself, felt it give a little under his weight.

A sudden surge of hope ran through him. He leaned on the stone arm harder and pushed. The arm moved now. As long as he leaned on the outer end of it, it bent down a little and he could push it in the other direction. That should open the door.

Clever work of those Mayas hundreds of years ago when they had built the temple. They had designed the door so that only those who knew how, could open and close it from the secret chamber.

He worked with all his might. Starting at the farthest end, he pushed it across the room, slowly, laboriously as far as it would go.

He caught hold of the edge of the hole in the roof and pulled himself out. It was growing darker now. He hurried down the carved steps in the back of the column the way he had come up.

There before him the stone door was open, even wider than it had been when he had first seen it. Luga dove inside. There was little light to show him the way. But he made out one figure near the door. He bent down and lifted the still form in his arms. It was Shakespeare.

He carried the body of the old actor outside and laid it on the paving in front of the entrance. Then he dove through the door and brought out another. That was the Bishop. Next he found the Key and last, King.

When he brought King out, the giant black staggered. Fear clutched at his heart. Perhaps something invisible had killed these friends of his. Something was making him weak and wobbly now. He managed to lay King's body on the paving, then he slumped beside him.

Things grew very hazy before his eyes. The entrance to the temple swam before him. He forced himself to take deep breaths of the clear, hot air about him and he felt a little better. Gradually, that weak feeling began to leave; his strength returned.

King was lying nearest him. He began to work over his master.

He had been taught the art of life saving in Cape Town where he had received his education. He was working it on King now.

It grew dark and he worked on. Fifteen minutes, a half hour slipped by. He felt King move a little; gradually he began to breathe more noticeably. He opened his eyes and stared up at Luga.

"Phew!" he said. "Thought we were done for, big boy. Where's—"

Luga pointed to the other three.

King struggled to his feet.

"I mean, where's Miss Waldorff?"

Luga shook his head.

"Sorry, Master," he said. "We come out of temple and Indians attack. I fight, but they hit me over the head with club and Luga not know anything more."

"You mean," King exploded, suddenly himself again, "that those red devils have taken her with them?"

"When I wake up," Luga said, "not find Miss Waldorff."

King's teeth clenched. He bent over the Key. "What did you do to revive me," he asked.

"What they teach to save drowning man," Luga said.

"Good," said King, "then work on the next one and I'll try to bring the Key back."

They worked in silence, King and his giant aide. Minutes passed. The Key was the first to show signs of coming back. Then the Bishop began breathing of his own accord.

"Must have been some kind of gas forced in that temple after the door went shut," King ventured.

Luga had a knife flashing in his right hand as he rushed toward the stake.

"Huh," stammered the Key. "Gas. You are out of gas. Got to land."

"You'll do," said King, leaving him to go to Shakespeare.

They worked on. The Key got to his feet and blinked. Luga explained how he had found the secret vault from which the door was operated.

"And you found the lid off of that room?" King asked.

"Yes, Master," said Luga. "Somebody work door shut from that room after we go inside temple. Luga see dirt on outside of column."

Shakespeare moved slightly. King kept on working. Luga came over to help him. The Bishop and the Key watched, still dizzy from their ordeal.

Suddenly King stopped and listened. Everyone tensed. Shakespeare took his first breath by himself.

From somewhere in the dusky darkness, the drone of a motor came to them.

"Jolly," exploded the Bishop, "they've stolen our plane."

King still listened, shook his head.

"If you mean because the sound seems to come from the lake, you might be wrong. The lake is behind the temple. And it may be the reflection of sound against the walls."

Shakespeare was breathing more easily. He sat up and coughed, glanced about at the tropical foliage and the carvings on the darkened temple and the starry heavens with a moon coming over the temple roof.

"Forsooth," he quoted, "I ne'er saw true beauty till this night."

"You'd have seen it in heaven," the Key chuckled, "in about two more hours, if your train across the river Styx was on time."

"I fear you are a bit confused, Key," said the Bishop twinkling. "The river Styx is crossed by a boat."

"This is a modern river Styx," the Key retorted. "Nowadays they got a railroad bridge and all. Believe me, I was on this side lookin' across a while ago. I know."

King shook his head. Apparently he hadn't heard the conversation at all. His face was set.

"Sounds like our engine," he said. "But we can't wait to find out now. The Indians have Connie Waldorff." He whirled to Luga. "Do you think we can trail them with a flashlight?"

"Yes, Master," nodded the faithful black.

King frowned, then turned to the entrance of the temple suddenly. "Wait," he said. "Want to check one thing."

He dived down the steps and looked between the two pillars where the leather bag had been placed.

"It's gone," he exclaimed. "They must have come down from that secret room while you were still out, Luga, taken the bag and gotten away. From the number of dead Indians around here, you sure put up a swell fight. Let's hope we're not too late."

LUGA TOOK the flashlight and hit the trail through the jungle. It was pitch dark now. Not even the bright beams of the moon filtered through the thick leaves of the forest about them.

The giant African was traveling at a half dog trot. The Bishop panted a little to keep up with the others. They plunged on regardless. Even King, in his wildest imagination, never dreamed what they would find at the other end of that long, fast trek through the forest.

Minute by minute they came closer. Now and then the trail led over rocks and Luga had to stop to make sure that he was still going in the right direction. Once he explained: "Luga not used to track men with flashlight."

On those stops the Bishop and Shakespeare got time to rest. Then they all plunged on and on.

An hour passed. King trailed behind to make sure that neither of the two older men dropped on the trail. He was getting plenty tired himself and marveled at their endurance.

Once he suggested, "Perhaps we'd better go a little slower."

"No," panted the Bishop. "I can—stand it—if Shakespeare can."

"You'll—not outrun me," the old actor challenged.

It was a long time after they left the temple when they saw something flickering through the trees ahead. A low cry from Luga warned them. Then they heard wild shouts from that lighted space.

The giant black slowed and crept warily toward the opening. They followed him with caution. They halted dead.

In the center of a small village several fires were lighted. Indians were dancing about a post in the middle. Dancing and yelling and howling. And now and then King saw one of them move closer to toss on another stick of firewood.

He recognized the whole thing at a glance and was struck with horror. The post was to be burned soon and tied against it was the limp form of Connie Waldorff.

Had they killed her already? He couldn't tell. Then a larger figure let out a wild yell and leaped into the circle. Dried twigs and branches were piled high about the girl so that her body was visible only from the waist up.

The large figure had a fire brand in his hand, and was waving it about. King tensed. "Let's go," he said. "Luga have you got a gun?"

"No. Got knife. Not gun now."

"Okay. The four of us will take care of the Indians. You knife anybody that gets in your way. Slash Connie Waldorff free, put her on your back and run like—like the very devil himself was after you."

"Yes, Master."

"Come on."

King leaped into the open. Luga was beside him. The Indians were dancing twice as fast as before; the throbbing of the drums increased to double time.

The chief was applying the brand of flame to the tinder about Connie's feet. The girl seemed to know nothing about it now.

Suddenly the nearest Indians saw what was coming. They turned and shouted a warning. There was a rush of wild confusion. Some came toward the five running men. Others fled in the opposite direction.

The chief was shouting wildly, waving his fire brand. Flames were already beginning to lick at the tinder brush pile surrounding Connie.

King fired at the Indian nearest to him. The Maya fell on his

195

face. Two others turned and fled. Another came on. King let go again with a well-aimed shot.

Blam! Blam!

The others were ring as they came running in. They broke through where the line of dancers had been, rushed the chief, who hesitated only a moment. Then he turned and fled.

King reached the stake a split second before any of the others. He kicked the pile of flaming sticks wide in every direction.

Luga had a knife flashing in his great right hand. An Indian leaped at him from the side. The knife gleamed in the firelight and the Indian screamed. Then the weapon came down with one swoop at the thongs that held Connie.

She slumped as she was freed and was about to pitch over in the burning embers.

Luga caught her with one great arm, tossed her over his shoulder like a bag of meal. He held her legs with his left arm and struck at two Indians who attacked him as he turned.

The knife gleamed red before he finished with those. They fell back, streaked with gushing blood and shrieking in mortal terror. LUGA WAS the first to go. He whirled from that last attack and dashed for the place in the side of the forest through which they had just come. The Bishop and Shakespeare followed him as closely as they could. But the giant black far outdistanced them even with the girl on his left shoulder.

The Key and King brought up the rear, running backward and shooting as they went.

Blam!

A rifle barked from the front of the chief's larger hut. King felt the breath of that bullet whisper in his ear as it passed.

Blam!

Another shot. This time it was closer. It all but nicked his ear. The Key let go with three shots at the chief, who went down shooting, hit apparently in the leg.

Yelping Indians were pouring now from the huts. Some of them carried clubs. A few had guns of various old vintages. They fired as King and the Key reached the cover of the woods.

"We've got to make fast time," King shouted. "Those Indians know these woods like a book. How's your sense of direction, Luga? Think you can strike a straight course to the lake?"

"Yes, Master."

"How—do—we—know," panted the Bishop. "That our plane is still there?"

"We don't," King answered. "We've got to take that chance. If it isn't there—"

"We're sunk," added the Key.

"If it isn't there," corrected King, "we'll have to do something else."

They were crashing through the darkness. Luga had the flashlight. At length he turned it on for a moment and turned it out again. A shot rang out from behind. The bullet whistled over their heads.

Even King was beginning to breathe harder. Someone crashed down ahead of him. It was Shakespeare.

"Don't mind me," gasped he old actor, "I'm done in as—the—"

"Like hell you are," cracked the Key.

The Bishop tried to correct his cursing but didn't have wind enough.

"Wait," King said as the Key tried to help the old actor to his feet. "I'll carry him. Here, give me your hand, Shakespeare."

He got the hand and swung the old actor over his shoulder.

"You watch the Bishop, Key," he ordered in a low voice. "See if you can help him over the rough spots."

"I'll—make it," the Bishop gasped.

"How much farther have we got to go?" Shakespeare panted over King's shoulder.

"Not very far," King lied.

Luga had slowed to let the others catch up. Now, closely bunched together, they rushed on. The giant black seemed to have an uncanny sense in the darkness. It was as though he had the eyes of a cat or a bat.

On and on they raced. King heard the Key's voice hissing in gasping tones back at him.

"Maybe we ought to stop and gang up on those redskins."

"That wouldn't do any good," King flung back. "They'd shoot from behind trees. They come like a bunch of cats. They don't make any more noise in these woods than Luga is making. It wouldn't surprise me if we were almost surrounded right now."

Then out of the darkness King heard Connie Waldorff's voice.

"Where—where are—"

That ended in a muffled gasp. Luga must have clapped his hand over her face. There was the sound of a muffled cry as though she were trying to cry out. Then all was still.

Luga had likely explained the situation to the girl.

There came a crash ahead, King stumbled and almost fell over something before him.

"The Bishop's down," said the Key.

A snort from Luga as he whirled.

"I carry the Bishop," he hissed.

"And Connie, too?" King gasped.

"Please," the girl whispered. "I'm sure I can make as good time as any of you. Please let me down and carry the Bishop instead."

"He's out cold," said the Key.

"Luga got him," the giant black said, swinging the heavy body of the Bishop over his shoulder and starting off as though he were empty handed.

The girl moved unsteadily at first beside King. He tried to help her although he was about all in himself carrying the old actor. Then he slowly found that the girl was helping to steady him. She was getting back her strength rapidly.

"I must have fainted," she panted as they trotted on. "Being tied to that pole was terrible. I was sure the end had come."

Crack!

Another bullet crashed through the branches above their heads. They came to a great wall and Luga swerved to the right now.

"Must be the temple," King panted. "Not much farther. Let's hope the plane is where we left it."

"What makes you think it might not be," the girl gasped.

"Heard a plane leave about three or four hours ago," King panted back. "Sounded like our engine. Maybe—fiend—behind this—got away in our plane. Your leather bag with the sand was gone."

Crack!

Another rifle bullet sang as it ripped through the woods beside them. Another and another cracked out and just missed one or the other of the running group.

Luga hissed back some words of encouragement.

"Not far to lake."

They would know the truth in another few minutes. They wobbled on now. Staggering. Connie Waldorff was almost holding King and his burden on his feet at times. Would that plane be there or would it be gone? King tried not to think of the alternative. At the lake, their backs would be to the wall, figuratively.

CHAPTER 19
VANISHING MEN

THE JUNGLE growth seemed to become more tangled and harder to plow through. Luga was picking his way the best he could in the darkness, but now even he was slowed by the heavier growth.

Crack!

Another and another shot rang out behind them and from right and left. The Indians had gained on them, but they weren't coming close enough to endanger themselves. They were trying to surround the party. They were even with them on each side now and closing in. No telling just how far that lake was ahead of them.

King's legs were about finished. He had plenty of strength usually, but the burden on his shoulder was too much for such a long distance. Shakespeare, while he was a tall gaunt man, weighed enough to make it very heavy going.

Twice Connie, who had hold of King's arm all of the time now, felt him sway as though he were going to fall. She did what she could to steady him.

"I—I wish I were stronger so that I could—" she gasped.

"Forget it," he panted— "and save your breath."

Then he heard a low shout from Luga just ahead. Heard the splash of water. They were at the lake. The terrible suspense was almost over. But was the plane there?

He heard Luga's voice.

"Plane here. Hurry!"

King broke through the thicker tangle at the lake edge and half fell in the water. He pitched Shakespeare into the door of the cabin. The old actor got to his feet and lurched to a seat.

King was fumbling in the darkness. He tried to get Connie in the plane next.

"No," she protested instantly. "You first. Get the engine started."

No time for argument. The girl seemed to mean what she said and it was the best way to save time.

A loud whoop came from the jungle as King dove through the door and rushed to slam in his seat. Connie was right behind him.

King whirred the starter. The engine caught and snorted out in the tropical night. The plane was shuddering from the pulsing of the great engine as it warmed. No time to wait for that though.

King whirled in the darkness of the cabin and shouted to Luga.

Blam—blam—blam!

That was the sound of a gun going off right at the cabin door. A scream of pain in the night and frantic thrashing about in the water of the lake.

"Everybody on board, Luga?"

A split second that seemed like endless time. What were those shots—from Indians or from King's men driving the Indians back?

Then Luga's answer came back.

"Yes, Master. Everybody in plane now. Hurry. Many Indians rushing us."

Blam—blam!

King kicked the throttle three-quarters open with the heel of his hand. He was still panting so hard that every breath was an effort and at the same time a blessing. Things swam a little before his eyes.

The motor of the low-winged job roared out in the night.

"Clear, Master," shouted Luga. "I cut ropes."

They were plowing out into the lake.

Crack—crack—crack!

Bullets drummed on the covering, but the plane was moving rapidly out of range.

FOR SOME time no one spoke. Everyone took it easy and got back their breath and their strength. Then, as they thundered across the neck of the Gulf of Mexico and up the Mexican coast, King turned to Connie.

"Just what did happen to you?"

She told him, with a little shudder once or twice. King listened, frowning.

"But who were they talking about?" he asked.

"I've been trying to figure that out ever since," Connie answered. "I feel sure it couldn't have been any of the Waldorffs."

"Did the chief describe this man to you?" he asked.

She nodded. "He said he was a big man. That's all. And that description would fit either my father, who is quite heavy, Uncle John, who is taller and leaner, and Cousin Henry, who—who was almost as tall as Uncle John and heavier. Even George, who is about his father's size."

Suddenly King straightened in his seat, snapped his fingers.

"It might be possible that some other person came down and told the Indians his name was Waldorff."

Connie considered that for a moment, then she shook her head.

"I don't know of any white man who knew our family history to that extent," she said. "Still, there might have been someone."

They hurled on as dawn broke.

They stopped once for gasoline, filled the tanks and raced on.

King swung his wireless sending key into operation. They had gained the United States and were flying over Texas. He began ticking off a message to the Doctor. Connie watched him.

"Just what are you doing now?" she asked.

"There is only one Waldorff left," King said. "I don't think your father could do this. He was struck by the curse–or rather the contents of the first two vials. So was your Uncle John. And your Cousin Henry was pronounced dead by the Doctor himself. That leaves only George. I'm radioing the Doctor for news and telling him to check on George. If George is not in New York, I think we're close to getting our man."

"I'm afraid you're right," she agreed. "I can't figure anyone else but George. Besides, he came down to Yucatan two or three years ago with his father."

"He was grown up then?" King asked.

The girl nodded. "He was—I think—twenty two and as big as he is now."

King fell silent and watched the radio light on the instrument panel. Minutes passed, then the light began to flicker. The earphones were already clamped on his head. The dots and dashes sputtered.

Learned last evening from Waldorff butler that George Waldorff left for Europe on the *Europa* to escape death from curse. Doctor

King repeated the message to Connie. Her eyes widened.

"I—I'm afraid it's Cousin George," she said, "but somehow I can't believe— Then our butler has returned."

"Apparently," said King. He sent another message. "I'm asking the Doctor to check the *Europa* by radio and find if George Waldorff can be positively identified as being on board."

They waited, tore on through morning skies. And as they flew, they ate a scant breakfast from the provisions on the plane.

It was a few minutes before they swooped down on the Nashville airport for gasoline and oil that they received an answer to King's last question.

George Waldorff positively identified as being on *Europa*. Doctor.

King and Connie simply stared at each other. King shrugged. "Well," he said, "that seems to settle that."

"Yes," the girl acknowledged. "It seems to. George couldn't have been in Yucatan and on board the *Europa* bound for Europe at the same time. Could he?"

King circled the airport and landed. After he gave his order to fill the tanks, they went to a lunch room to eat. When he returned, he found the airport manager waiting for him.

"Staying long here?" he asked.

"No," said King.

"Better stay over for the afternoon," the man went on. "We've got an air circus coming off and there's a prize of five hundred dollars for the winner of the free-for-all race. That bus of yours ought to win hands down."

King glanced about. The airport had a deserted look, not at all as if races were taking place in an hour or so. The manager, evidently, was just stalling to keep them there until he could make a complete check on the plane number.

"Sorry," said King, "but we've got to push through." He lowered his voice to confidential tones. "This is a police plane from New York. We're chasing a ship we believe just left Yucatan. The numbers are very similar. The last number of our plane is a 3 and the last number of their plane is an 8. You haven't seen them go through, have you?"

He saw he had the manager wondering for a moment; then the man shook his head.

"Haven't seen a sign of it," he said, "but we got your message to be on the look-out for the plane."

"Good," approved King. "Keep your eye peeled. You'd better get some police out here to handle them. They're tough customers."

"I will," said the manager. "And glad to have seen you."

King paid for the gas. The others climbed into the cabin as the manager watched. He wasn't very certain of himself, and before he could decide, the cabin job was in the air again.

Through the whole afternoon they sped across the States. It was growing dusk when they reached the metropolitan area. King swung to the right of the city and kept going. Here and there he saw a plane in the air. The nearest swung toward him as though to head him off.

Deliberately, King swung due east out to sea. He glanced back out of the window several times. Planes were following. THEY FLEW the length of Long Island and then out on the Atlantic. It grew dark. When he was out of sight of land, King swung in a wide circle and came back toward the north shore.

It was night now and pitch black except for the moon. With the help of its light, he was able to locate the hidden field near their cabin.

Several moments later he was hurrying through the cabin

door. The first thing to catch his eyes was a slip of white paper lying on the table.

Have gone to Waldorff Mansion to look things over.

Doctor King folded the note and stuffed it into his pocket.

"It looks," he said, "as though that's our next stop. We've got to take you home, Connie, and the Doctor must have found something at your house that needed investigating."

Connie hesitated. "You're going to drive in a car?" she asked.

"I think," said King, "we'll take two cars. Key, suppose you and Shakespeare take the roadster. Meet us at the Waldorff home. Shakespeare, it might be well to take along your make-up case. We don't know what we're going to run into. The rest of us will go in the—"

He stopped short.

"I nearly forgot," he said. "If the Doctor has gone to town, he's probably taken his sedan. That will force us to all go in the roadster."

"I think I could help a little," said Connie. "I can fly my plane back to Roosevelt Field and take a train in from there."

King nodded. "Not a bad idea," he said. They started out of the cabin. "We'll meet you at your house."

At the little airport he started her engine for her. The girl settled in the cockpit, warmed the engine, then she was thundering into the air and turning west.

When the others reached the place where the cars were usually hidden, they had a surprise. The Doctor had taken the roadster, leaving the sedan for them.

King took the wheel. The Bishop and Shakespeare and Luga and the Key crowded into the other seats. They got into motion.

As they rolled down the main highway to the west, the Bishop raised a question.

"Would it be possible," he said, "for this liquid in the vials to render the—er—subjects physically fit and still have their brains non-performing? What I mean to say, perhaps have their brains so dulled that they were controlled by the hypnotic powers of others?"

"I've been trying to figure that out myself," said King. "I'll tell you something that gave me the idea. When we found James Waldorff outside the vault, he read my thought twice before I spoke."

"Holy gee," muttered the Key. "What dough that guy could make if—"

"I hardly think he needs money," Shakespeare cut in, "but no doubt from a theatrical standpoint, it would be—er—"

"Jolly," exclaimed the Bishop, "it would seem that you have solved the problem. If the brains of men who have had two doses of those vials, become tuned to the brains of others, their acts and words could be controlled by another, perhaps in the same room."

"Come to think of it," King said, "that's what it did seem like. And that's what has made me suspect George Waldorff. Remember when old John Flint was coming up the cellar stairs? The minute George entered the hall and called to his father, the footsteps stopped. There must have been some break in the hypnotic influence."

Traffic was growing heavier. They were coming into the city. They crossed the bridge, turned downtown, through Central Park and then they were pulling up before the Waldorff Mansion.

They found Connie Waldorff waiting for them on the steps, standing in the shadow.

"I made good time," she said, "just got here myself. One of the boys I know at Roosevelt flew me to Floyd Bennett and it didn't take long from there."

She was walking to the front door as she spoke. She took a key from the pocket of her riding breaches and unlocked the door. A wild-eyed butler met them. Connie frowned at him.

"I thought you were leaving for good, Harvey," she said.

The butler bowed, seemed embarrassed.

"I—I'm afraid I fully intended to, Miss Constance," he replied, "but when I got away, I was ashamed of myself so I came back to see it through, if you know what I mean."

"That was brave of you," Connie said. "Has anything happened since I've been gone?"

At that moment the butler spied Luga. His eyes almost popped out of his head. His face went white.

"This," Connie explained, "is Luga. A friend of mine. He saved my life scarcely twenty-four hours ago. Has anything happened or anyone been here, Harvey?

Harvey blinked twice, gulped and nodded.

"Yes, ma'am," he said. "The Doctor who came with that gentleman—" pointing to King—"came quite a bit ago. He went into the library and said he wanted to be left alone there.

He closed the door. I believe you'll find him there now, Miss Constance. He hasn't come out."

Connie Waldorff turned to the library, opened the door—stopped stock still in the doorway.

"Why, Harvey," she exclaimed, "there's no one here!"

King rushed past her and stared about. The library was empty as a deserted barn. Not a sign of a living thing. Then he spied a piece of paper lying on the table.

Come to 12 ½ E. 55 Street at once. I need help. Walk right in. Hurry. Doctor.

He compared the note with the other one in his pocket, nodded with satisfaction.

"It's the Doctors handwriting all right," he said.

CHAPTER 20
THE BAT-MAN

CONNIE WALDORFF took the message and stared at it, then looked up at King, puzzled.

"That's strange," she said, "that house is just around the corner. In fact, my father owns it. It's been vacant for some time and is to be torn down for an apartment building."

She spun 'round and faced the butler angrily.

"Harvey," she snapped, "you're lying to me. The Doctor did leave the library. He couldn't get out any other way."

Harvey's face took on a hurt look.

"Beggin' your pardon, Miss Constance," he said, "I've been

about the hall for the past two hours, ever since the Doctor went into the library alone and closed the door. I thought you would wish me to. And I swear the Doctor has not gone out of the library, at least through the door into the hall."

King was halfway to the front door. He reached it and opened it.

"We're going over to that house," he said.

Outside, they piled into the sedan, King at the wheel again. He drove hallway down the block and slowed.

"Isn't that the roadster?" he asked.

"Jolly, it is," said the Bishop.

"The Doctor didn't want to park in front of the house," King said. "Key, you get out and follow us in it."

The Key leaped out, got into the roadster and followed around the corner. King pulled up before a house that was tightly shuttered and looked as though it hadn't been lived it in years. He parked directly in front of it and from the protection of the car, studied the street for a moment. He spoke low to the others.

"Across the street," he said, "I can just make out two figures under that high stairs on the front of that house. I think they're watching this place."

"Looks like a trap to me," whispered the Key, who had joined them again.

"Right," said King, "but we've got to go through with it. The Doctor says he needs us and we're going to help him if we can."

He paused a minute and shot a glance over the others.

"Connie," he decided, "I think you and Shakespeare better go with me. Just a hunch. And the rest of you, Luga and Bishop and Key, go for a walk around the block. Then come back. Come back singly. And keep an eye on those two across the street."

With that, King turned. Half bent over, he moved up the long brownstone steps as though he were hobbling. Shakespeare and the girl came behind him.

He reached the top of the steps, turned slightly. The two men in the shadow across the street were still standing.

King put his hand on the knob and turned. The door opened with a ghastly squeaking sound that echoed through the empty house.

He tensed there a moment and tried to see into the darkness. As he felt for a light, he had a strange feeling that there were more in that hall than just he and Connie and Shakespeare.

He took four steps inside, Connie and Shakespeare were right behind him. Then—*Wham!*

The door closed with a muffled sound.

A cry came from Connie Waldorff.

King whirled as a light went on in the hall. A very dim light. But he could see things in it all too plainly.

Standing with its back to the door, stood a weird thing. It was much like the giant paper and metal bat that had attacked them in the Temple of Azrah. But this was smaller, about the size of a man. The face was like the other—half man, half bat.

Connie had cried out when she had touched the thing. King sprang at it only to instantly draw back.

A member like a claw protruded from somewhere at the middle of the body. And in that claw was a gleaming automatic. Great wings were folded back against the shoulders of the beastlike thing.

King chilled as the monster spoke in a plainly disguised, singsong voice. But there was something in that voice that he thought he could recognize.

"You will go down the hall. Your friends await you—there."

The three moved before the advance of the bat-man. Moved step by step. They came to a door at the back.

"Open—the—door," ordered the bat-man.

King put his hand on the knob.

He heard Connie gasp as they entered a lighted room. Three figures were seated in chairs. Three figures that slumped back with heads cast down on their chests.

There was John Flint Waldorff, James Waldorff and the Doctor.

A harsh, cackling laugh came from the batman.

"Your friends are here," he repeated. "Are you not glad to see them?"

Then, before their bulging eyes, the Doctor began to rise unnaturally from his chair. With his head still down on his chest, he began to speak.

"I have investigated the Maya curse," he said very slowly. "I have found that it exists. I am a man of science. I know. You cannot fool the Maya curse. You left a bag of sand instead of money at the temple. The curse god is very angry. He will kill us all if you, Constance Waldorff, do not give him the ten million. He will give you one more chance to leave the money at the temple."

213

The Doctor sat down wearily.

King's teeth clenched. He glanced at the blue steel of the automatic in the bat-man's hand.

"What is your answer?" sang the bat-man.

Connie Waldorff stood rigid. She seemed to be trying to think.

"Perhaps you need urging," said the bat-man. "I will tell you then. There on that table, you see three carved vials. Those belong to me. The one on the left brings death. The one in the middle brings life back to the body but renders the brain mine. The third will make a man entirely well."

King stared at those three precious vials. Death. Semi-life and full life.

Then King noticed that the glowing eyes of the bat-man were glaring at him.

"You are King," said the weird voice. "I have no use for you. I will put you out of the front door again. There you will die."

"Turn and go down the hall," he ordered. "And take your old friend with the funny box under his arm along with you. You will both die."

King turned. There was something about that automatic pistol in the hand of the bat-man that wouldn't take an argument.

THEY MOVED together down the darker hall toward the front door. King was thinking quickly. He made a wild guess. Those two men across the street were thugs hired to kill him.

King was walking on the left. Shakespeare was on his right. The ghastly bat-man was directly behind, with his gun in King's back. One false move and King would be dead. But perhaps with luck—-

They reached the front door and stopped. King spoke in a low voice, "Maybe you think you're kidding the rest, Henry Waldorff, but not me."

"You think I am Henry Waldorff," said the other. "But Henry Waldorff died before your eyes."

"You made it look like that," King snapped back, "but it's plenty clear now. You had some substance on your throat that darkened with the air. Then you slumped in your chair and the Doctor said your heart had stopped beating. I can see how that could have been faked easily."

There was a moment of pause. Then the batman answered in a low voice.

"All right, I am Henry Waldorff, then. But that will not help you, you meddlesome fool. When I force you and your old friend out of the front door, my men across the street will riddle you with machine guns."

King's brain spun. He had guessed somewhere near right there.

"I imagine," he said calmly, "that it's going to be quite a shock to you to know that my men outside have captured your two thugs and Luga, my black Zulu aide, has choked them to death."

He felt the automatic waver.

King's muscles tensed. With lightning speed, he whirled to the right.

Blam!

The gun exploded—but not in his back. It scorched his side. A

With his head still down on his chest, the Doctor began

to speak, while the bat-man held them at bay.

cry came from Connie Waldorff. King's left fist crashed against the false face of the bat-man, and it fell off. Henry Waldorff staggered back.

But that loaded automatic was waving about in the air.

Slowly, Waldorff bore down King's arm. Got him in a strong grip that shut off the feeling from the hand that clutched his gun arm. King was losing inch by inch.

He shook his right free and crashed it to Waldorff's face again with all his might. Then he felt Henry stiffen in his grasp, and he heard Connie snap out an order.

"One more move from you, Cousin Henry, and I'll pull the trigger of this gun."

King wrested the gun from Waldorff, stuck it against his side. Connie stepped back and dropped her empty hand.

King stared at it. The girl had saved the day by sticking a crooked finger hard in her cousin's back.

"Nice work, Connie," King panted. "Now, Henry, we'll take a little walk down the hall again."

Henry turned stiffly. Halfway down the hall, a forced laugh came from him.

"I hope you don't take me too seriously," he said. "I was only having a little fun with those three vials I found in the Maya temple three years ago. It was my men who took John Flint from the ambulance. It was I who broke in and raised your father, Constance, from the dead. Manaha was an easy one to turn suspicion upon. He's safe in the secret passage that leads from the mansion to this house. A panel opens into it from the library. You open it by pressing a button in the carving of the fireplace mantle. And when you thought I died in the library—I had a very clever shield that fitted over my heart so that the doctor could not feel it beating."

"And I suppose you were the one who boarded John Flint's yacht with the police and took a half million dollars from the safe," King grinned as he forced Henry into the back room. "Ha-ha-ha. That was a good joke. Well, now the turn fits on the other foot.... Lie down on the floor."

"W—what are going to do with me?" stammered Henry Waldorff.

"Just a harmless little joke," King chuckled. "Shakespeare, go to work on him. Make him look like me. We'll put my clothes on him. And Connie, take his gun. I imagine you'd get a kick out of shooting him if he moved."

Connie Waldorff's mouth was set in a hard little straight line.

"I certainly would," she nodded. She took the gun.

"Hurry it up, Shakespeare," King said.

"I'll do my best," the old actor promised.

While he worked, and Connie held Henry at the point of her gun, King whirled and leaped for the three carved vials on the table.

He tried to remember which was which. The middle one brought the dead men partially back to life. The one on the end restored them completely—but which end? He spun 'round to Henry Waldorff.

"It's the one on the right that brings them back, isn't it?" he demanded.

"Ye—yes," stammered the terror-stricken man. "Believe me.

It was only a joke. I wanted to see how it would work. We would all have had a good laugh about it later."

"You're a liar," King snapped. "How big a dose do I give them?"

"A—a few drops on the tongue is enough," said Henry Waldorff. "I beg of you. Don't kill me. I tell you it was—"

"Shut up," King cracked.

He picked up the carved vial on the right, uncorked it, and stepped over to James Waldorff. He tilted the head back and poured a few drops of the liquid into his mouth. James gulped.

Next he went to John Flint and did the same to him. Then the Doctor. By the time he had administered the drops to the Doctor, James Waldorff was showing strange signs. He began to stiffen. Then his head came up slowly. And there was a natural look about his eyes that King had not seen there before. He blinked and stared about him like a man waking suddenly from a very sound sleep.

He stared at King in bewilderment, noticed his own daughter standing over her cousin with a gun.

"Constance," he exclaimed. "What is going on here?"

"I'd rather tell you about it when everything is over," said the girl, shifting her eyes once to see that her father was all right. "You're sure you are fully awake, father'?" she asked fearfully.

"Why—why, of course," said her father. "But—"

God," Connie breathed.

John Flint was taking on life. And so was the Doctor. They sat up and stared about them. Stared at each other. Then the Doctor smiled.

"I remember being surprised after I found the secret passage out of the library," he said. "How long have I been—dead?"

"About two or three hours," said King tearing the bat robe from Henry Waldorff. He stared at a dark gray suit something like his own. "That suit will do as well as mine," he decided. "And your face, Henry. How much you resemble me now!"

Henry Waldorff showed white under the ears where the make-up had not changed his appearance.

"What—what are you going to do with me?" he cried.

"I'm going to take you and set you free," King smiled. "As free as your plans will let you be."

Henry Waldorff's whole expression changed.

"I must say," he said, "that is fine of you. You realize, of course, that the whole thing was a joke. Yes, indeed. John, James, I hope you're feeling fit and well again?"

But the two didn't have a chance to answer before something happened. Henry struck with his right hand. And in that thrust, he knocked the gun from Connie's fingers. Then he leaped at the vials and snatched at all three of them.

THE DOCTOR sprang forward. But King was there before him. His left and then his right flashed to Henry Waldorff's stomach and jaw in turn.

Henry was hurled back. His arms went up and his hands released the vials.

King was trying to catch all three of them. But he couldn't make it. He caught one-the one that brought men back to full life. The other two crashed to the floor and broke in a million pieces of pottery. The liquid they contained spilled down into the boards.

Connie had regained the gun that was knocked from her hand. She held it now against her cousin's back as the Doctor locked his arms in his powerful grasp.

"I'd like very much to see you knock this gun out of my hand again," said Connie sagely.

King turned to James and John Waldorff. He handed the one vial to John Flint Waldorff.

"Mr. Waldorff," he said, "you're doubtless pretty hazy about what has been going on, but your niece will explain later. However, I'd like to give you this. There are a number of Maya Indians about ten miles south of the Temple of Azrah to whom the contents of this bottle will mean life, poor devils. I thought you'd like to carry out that mission."

John Flint nodded.

"I haven't the least idea what you're talking about, young man," he said, "but if my niece is connected with it, I'm sure it must be above-board. I'll do as she wishes."

"Swell," said King. He turned and took the gun from Connie. "If you'll try to explain to your father and uncle," he said, "I'll take care of setting your Cousin Henry free."

Connie stared at him strangely for a moment. Then she must have read his thoughts for she nodded.

"Very well."

King prodded Henry with the gun.

"Down the hall," he ordered.

Henry moved along the hall without argument. But as they neared the door, he stopped short.

"Good Lord, man," he demanded, "you're not going to make me go out of that front door?"

King smiled. "Right," he nodded. "Just like you were going to send me out. Nice little trap you laid for yourself."

"But—but," stammered Henry Waldorff, "you said that your men had captured my thugs."

"I'm very sorry," said King sagely, "but I lied to you."

Henry Waldorff turned to plead. But King was already opening the door. The Doctor gave a brutal shove.

Henry Waldorff shot through the opening to the top steps. King slammed the door and darted back against the wall. He pushed the Doctor against the opposite wall of the hall.

From outside came a cry—but it came too late, for it was cut off by the stutter of machine guns. Flying steel slashed against the heavy wood door. Then all was still.

Gingerly, King opened the door and peered out.

"Doctor," he called. "Look."

The door opened wider. They stood there staring together.

A giant black form had leaped from the rail of the steps above where the two men were crouched in the shadow with their machine guns. It was dark, but King could see those giant arms flailing. And even at that distance, he could hear the snap and crack as Luga broke the backs of the thugs, one over each knee. King raced to the back of the hall.

"Hurry," he shouted, "We haven't a minute to waste. The police will be here any second."

223

Everyone rushed headlong for the entrance. They were joined in front by the Bishop and the Key and Luga.

They piled into the sedan and roadster. King, at the wheel of the sedan, shot her into gear and they darted down the street just as they heard the siren of a police car.

But that police car never saw them, for they turned the corner. Police would find the dead body of Henry Waldorff with a face like that of King of The Secret 6 and bullet holes sieving his body.

And they would find two gunmen on the opposite side of the street with their backs broken.

King drew up before the Waldorff Mansion.

"Young man," said James Waldorff, "from what Constance has told me, you have done a wonderful thing for us. How can I repay you?"

King smiled.

"It's been a real pleasure, Mr. Waldorff," he said. "And that's the truth. But if you mean financially, I've always had an idea I'd like to endow a large farm for city orphans. You know, the country is the place to bring up youngsters, anyway."

Mr. Waldorff nodded. "You draw up the plans and let me know when you want money."

"Thanks," said King. "That's mighty fine of you. But we've got to shove off now before the cops come around."

He felt Connie's hand on his arm.

"It doesn't seem right to let you go—like this," she said softly. "After—everything."

"You wouldn't want me to get arrested would you?" King laughed.

Then he was gone.

Connie Waldorff must have told the entire story of her adventures that night to old John Flint.

For next morning about eleven o'clock, the yacht, *Pagan,* plowed the waves close to the north shore of Long Island, bound for Yucatan. And the six men on shore saw John Flint Waldorff and his faithful servant, Manaha, standing on the forward deck. The yacht even came close enough so they could see John Flint pull the rope that sounded the whistle—6 short blasts, a salute to let King and his Secret 6 know how grateful he was.

THE SPIDER

- ❑ #1: The Spider Strikes — $13.95
- ❑ #2: The Wheel of Death — $13.95
- ❑ #3: Wings of the Black Death — $13.95
- ❑ #4: City of Flaming Shadows — $13.95
- ❑ #5: Empire of Doom! — $13.95
- ❑ #6: Citadel of Hell — $13.95
- ❑ #7: The Serpent of Destruction — $13.95
- ❑ #8: The Mad Horde — $13.95
- ❑ #9: Satan's Death Blast — $13.95
- ❑ #10: The Corpse Cargo — $13.95
- ❑ #11: Prince of the Red Looters — $13.95
- ❑ #12: Reign of the Silver Terror — $13.95
- ❑ #13: Builders of the Dark Empire — $13.95
- ❑ #14: Death's Crimson Juggernaut — $13.95
- ❑ #15: The Red Death Rain — $13.95
- ❑ #16: The City Destroyer — $13.95
- ❑ #17: The Pain Emperor — $13.95
- ❑ #18: The Flame Master — $13.95
- ❑ #19: Slaves of the Crime Master — $13.95
- ❑ #20: Reign of the Death Fiddler — $13.95
- ❑ #21: Hordes of the Red Butcher — $13.95
- ❑ #22: Dragon Lord of the Underworld — $13.95
- ❑ #23: Master of the Death-Madness — $13.95
- ❑ #24: King of the Red Killers — $13.95
- ❑ #25: Overlord of the Damned — $13.95
- ❑ #26: Death Reign of the Vampire King — $13.95
- ❑ #27: Emperor of the Yellow Death — $13.95
- ❑ #28: The Mayor of Hell — $13.95
- ❑ #28: Slaves of the Murder Syndicate — $13.95

THE MYSTERIOUS WU FANG

- ❑ #1: The Case of the Six Coffins — $12.95
- ❑ #2: The Case of the Scarlet Feather — $12.95
- ❑ #3: The Case of the Yellow Mask — $12.95
- ❑ #4: The Case of the Suicide Tomb — $12.95
- ❑ #5: The Case of the Green Death — $12.95
- ❑ #6: The Case of the Black Lotus — $12.95
- ❑ #7: The Case of the Hidden Scourge — $12.95

G-8 AND HIS BATTLE ACES

- ❑ #1: The Bat Staffel — $13.95

CAPTAIN SATAN

- ❑ #1: The Mask of the Damned — $13.95
- ❑ #2: Parole for the Dead — $13.95
- ❑ #3: The Dead Man Express — $13.95
- ❑ #4: A Ghost Rides the Dawn — $13.95
- ❑ #5: The Ambassador From Hell — $13.95

THE SECRET 6

- ❑ 1: The Red Shadow — $13.95
- ❑ **NEW:** #2: House of Walking Corpses — $13.95

CAPTAIN ZERO

- ❑ #1: City of Deadly Sleep — $13.95
- ❑ #2: The Mark of Zero! — $13.95
- ❑ #3: The Golden Murder Syndicate — $13.95

OPERATOR 5

- ❑ #1: The Masked Invasion — $13.95
- ❑ #2: The Invisible Empire — $13.95
- ❑ #3: The Yellow Scourge — $13.95
- ❑ #4: The Melting Death — $13.95
- ❑ #5: Cavern of the Damned — $13.95
- ❑ #6: Master of Broken Men — $13.95
- ❑ #7: Invasion of the Dark Legions — $13.95
- ❑ #8: The Green Death Mists — $13.95
- ❑ #9: Legions of Starvation — $13.95
- ❑ #10: The Red Invader — $13.95
- ❑ #11: The League of War-Monsters — $13.95
- ❑ #12: The Army of the Dead — $13.95
- ❑ #13: March of the Flame Marauders — $13.95
- ❑ #14: Blood Reign of the Dictator — $13.95
- ❑ #15: Invasion of the Yellow Warlords — $13.95

DUSTY AYRES AND HIS BATTLE BIRDS

- ❑ #1: Black Lightning! — $13.95
- ❑ #2: Crimson Doom — $13.95
- ❑ #3: The Purple Tornado — $13.95
- ❑ #4: The Screaming Eye — $13.95
- ❑ #5: The Green Thunderbolt — $13.95
- ❑ #6: The Red Destroyer — $13.95
- ❑ #7: The White Death — $13.95
- ❑ #8: The Black Avenger — $13.95
- ❑ #9: The Silver Typhoon — $13.95
- ❑ #10: The Troposphere F-S — $13.95
- ❑ #11: The Blue Cyclone — $13.95
- ❑ #12: The Tesla Raiders — $13.95

DR. YEN SIN

- ❑ #1: Mystery of the Dragon's Shadow — $12.95
- ❑ #2: Mystery of the Golden Skull — $12.95
- ❑ #3: Mystery of the Singing Mummies — $12.95

MAVERICKS

- ❑ #1: Five Against the Law — $12.95
- ❑ #2: Mesquite Manhunters — $12.95
- ❑ #3: Bait for the Lobo Pack — $12.95
- ❑ #4: Doc Grimson's Outlaw Posse — $12.95
- ❑ #5: Charlie Parr's Gunsmoke Cure — $12.95